wisteria, vol. I

Also by R. D. G. Lover

Angels' Compass
Tempest of Angels
Inheriting Armageddon

The Tides of Amelia Island
The Storm & the Sea
Rose Tide & Rust

the wisteria collection
wisteria, vol. I

Coloring Books
The Amelia Island Coloring Book

wisteria, vol. I

a collection of fiction & poetry

r. d. g. lover

4pocalypse Arts

4pocalypse Arts

This book is a work of fiction. Any references to historical events, real people, or real places are used fictitiously. Other names, characters, places, and events are product of the author's imagination, and any resemblance to actual events or places or persons, living or dead, is entirely coincidental.

First Paperback Edition March 2025

For information about special discounts for bulk purchases or to book an event with the author, please contact R. D. G. Lover at www.4pocalypsearts.com or via email at racheldglover@gmail.com.

ISBN 979-8-9904778-3-4

for all the nights I spent dreaming,
for all the longings and love that I poured into that dream,
and for the ones I loved along the way:
for Lucy,
for my lover,
for the friends I made at the tide line,

and most importantly,
for the person I've become.

table of contents

author's note

In folklore, wisteria is often considered to be a portal to different worlds because it likes to grow on doorways.

Writing has taken me to many different worlds that include hardware stores full of magical women and giants, intervention interviews, lethal offices, and poisoned wine.

I have a handful of stories I'm very fond of that I think are worth sharing. There's something for everyone in this collection: fiction, suspense, humor, satire, a touch of romance, fantasy, and poetry too. So, without further ado…

Welcome to my worlds.
I hope you enjoy your stay.

no one

No one loves like
an artist does.

love potion

My love potion
is made of blood, sweat, and tears.

For years
I poured myself out
    into
        you
    my art
my love
    my beating,
bleeding
        heart.

My love potion is
the cider beside my desk
for days I have to drink
to seduce the muse;

My love potion is
the tears I've wept
in search of meaning
for the callousness
of those who should care;

My love potion is
the callous on my middle finger:
a telltale sign
        of the minutes
                the hours
                the days
                        the decade
I've spent honing this dream
        my skill
my passion.

My love potion is *you*
the one who
                listens
the one who
                sees
the work I've put into these stories
the truth behind these stories, too,
the truth that is *me*.

Drama & the Muse

The Muse was beautiful. No matter the shape she took, she inspired any who saw her. She often took on the image of the Greek Muses, too, to entertain the lore surrounding her. She would be fair-skinned and dark-haired, and her eyes would hold worlds within them.

She called herself simply "Muse," a fitting name. Anyone she told it to told her it suited her.

Muse lived at peace with most everyone she met. She walked slowly when she went through parks, making sure to look in the direction of the boy with his notepad, sketching a metal statue. She looked, too, at the couple sitting on the stone bench beneath the trees, who sat still as stone, to watch squirrels and pigeons approach. The girl there would be inspired; she would write about it someday.

Muse didn't usually speak to those she inspired, just observed. That's what Muse thought was best: observing. If you observed, you were a true artist. You saw the things others overlooked—the emotion slipping from a stranger's eye, the adolescent girl who tap-dances for hardware store checkout cameras, the way that snowflakes perch on black and demand to be appreciated, the toy cars on a young college boy's dresser…

Muse liked those things. They told a lot about people.

Most all that Muse did was observe, in fact. But sometimes being mindful and watchful got her into trouble. People noticed that Muse watched. People watched Muse, too. One of those was Drama.

Drama had many, many names. They had many, many faces, too. Drama liked that about themself. Many faces meant many stories; Muse agreed but in a very different way. Perhaps it was true that Drama and Muse were two sides of the same coin. Muse went about planting stories and inspiration, let the idea make a ripple effect on its own. But Drama got right in front of you, told you what you *should* believe, making a splash in their wake. No one escaped the waves they made.

Muse did not like Drama.

But Drama loved the Muse.

Drama thought, should they get in front of Muse enough, should they talk and talk and talk and talk, that their ideas would inspire the Muse. Drama would *compel* the Muse. *Of course,* they thought. *All good inspiration from the Muse comes from Drama, from us. She needs us to create, she needs us to be. She needs us.*

Muse did not feel the same.

There was enough in the world around her, Muse thought, that she could work with. Small things inspire large things. Large things inspire small things. All without doing damage.

Drama did damage.

Drama spread rumors. Drama told lies when they needed to. Drama shamed the confident and beautiful to feel good about themselves. Drama withheld the work promotion. Drama threw away business cards. Drama didn't inspire; Drama hindered. But it made for good stories. At least, that's how Drama saw it.

Muse couldn't quite disagree. Here she was, writing about Drama after all. Drama had forced their way in front of the Muse. Drama demanded to be seen.

Muse was tired of it. After a while, she decided, she *would* use the stories Drama shoved her way. They would not be stories Drama liked.

So it was final, that if Muse and Drama were two sides of the same coin, one side would be Universal Truth and the other would be Satire.

hope is a tricky thing

I lost the voice I used to sing

and it stings,

the brush of a fleeting dream;
the paper edge of a wound;
the blood on my fingertips;
    the blood I used—
to ink the lyrics, the story,

the fiend.

You tricked me,
you evil thing:
    dreams,
ambition, and hope.

I laid to rest the fire in my soul.

Once it was raging.
Twice it was a flame.
It was an ember, too,
kindling and shy.
It almost went out.

I fanned the flame until I burned my hands
    scars on my fingerprints,
                        removed.
Scars on my arms,
            the hollow wound.

It was all supposed to make sense.
It was all supposed to make it worth it.
All the pain
    my child shoulders carried—
all the generational grief, the greed,
the way I twisted and bent and broke

                into pieces.

I took ink and gold
and glued myself together.

I took the fragments of my soul
—jagged and marred—
and created solemn reflections
which smiled for me,
        …eventually.

We smiled together.
    We celebrated together.
We won wars together.

We took on our demons,
        and we won(!)

But hope is a tricky thing.

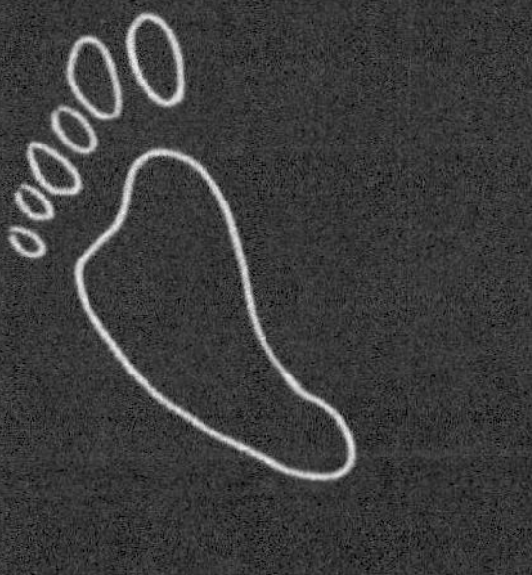

The Story of the Sixth Toe

James had a thing for playing pranks. It wasn't really his fault, if you asked him. You see, he lived a painfully normal life in a painfully normal town with painfully *boring* people. Everyone was always saying, "Do your job," and "Play your part," and "Behave." *Behave* was everyone's favorite word in James's town.

James was tired of always behaving. He was the ripe age of seventeen, and danger always called his name. Danger was his lover, his middle name. And with the brightest blond hair and the prettiest face in town, danger found him fast. A mix of danger, crude humor, and pranks made any day a good day for James. Innocent humor was just *okay*. It was the type of humor his best friends gravitated towards, and it was a quick fix, a grain of sugar when he craved a whole cube. Still, he would take it when it was offered.

James's best friends were Benjamin and Ryan. They were goody-two-shoes boys who always had their sights on good girls and politeness and apprenticeships that could get them far in life. James thought it was pretty silly. Benjamin had a good apprenticeship secured already; he was a squire, a knight in training. Ryan was a blacksmith, always making prettier things than the rest of the men in the village. The other men wrote Ryan off for it, saying that "Beautiful is not practical." James had a lot of respect for Ryan because Ryan never let those stupid things said about his work stop him. But James was just the village idiot.

Still, at the end of the day, James, Benjamin, and Ryan were boys, and boys will be boys.

Today started like most other days did. Benjamin and Ryan had their lunch breaks, covered in sweat and silt respectively. James met them there tossing an apple from hand to hand. One of them mentioned that a local farmer was looking for an apprentice, but James brushed it off then tossed each of them an apple. They weren't stolen; Benjamin had asked this the first time James showed up with three, ruby-red apples. James got his apples from the market, and he traded stories for the goodies. The girl at the market was sweet, with eyes and hair like chocolate and a voice as smooth as it, too. When James first explained this, Ryan told him that that girl had eyes for James. James brushed that off, too.

"I heard the town is pouring new concrete around the town's temple," Benjamin said. He took a bite of his apple.

"I heard, too," Ryan said. He eyed Benjamin with sea-glass green eyes. "My master has me and the others moving wooden boards to make the edges of the pour clean. Said it's happening tonight."

"Tonight," James mused.

Benjamin looked at James with a very plain, very deadpan, very *charged* expression. Benjamin's expressions were always like that. The less an emotion showed on his face, the more the emotion built up on the inside. Benjamin was usually the first one to jump to stop James from plotting anything too extreme.

"I have an idea," James said.

"No," Benjamin said before James could explain his idea.

James continued as if Benjamin hadn't said anything at all. "After they pour the concrete—after dark—we sneak back out and walk through it and leave tracks. We can draw penises, too."

This time, Ryan said, "*No.*"

James rolled his eyes. "It's harmless fun."

"It's *rude*. You don't even know how much time goes into something like that, James," Ryan said.

James didn't really care how much time went into something like that.

Lunch ended quickly, and James didn't mind that. Benjamin and Ryan didn't seem too interested in drawing penises on newly poured concrete for the whole town to admire anyway. What James was worried about was that they would try to stop him, because James *did* plan to go out after dark.

James spent his afternoon watching the sun sway across the sky, splayed on his back under a tree on the outskirts of town. He thought about lots while he was there. Mostly, he told himself stories, or rather, his brain told him stories. He enjoyed the wandering of his mind. It always did funny things, like showing him a teetering spin top that looked like a pirate's steering wheel or a circle of strange tarot cards with even stranger, glowing etchings on them. His brain played tricks on things like that. He was never quite sure what he was seeing in his brain, but he was pretty sure he could call it creativity. It was the same whorls of colors and things and words he saw when he told stories—of adventure, of horror, of romance— to the sweet girl at the produce market. James realized he really, *really* liked stories.

When the sun set on the horizon, James was thinking about footprints and the kinds of stories they could tell—of wandering nomads, of fleeing slaves, of runaway children, of boys and girls who found peace in the night and quiet.

The town was dark and quiet, and James himself found a lot of peace in that. The market stands had rugged sacks thrown over mounds of produce and other goods. Curtains were drawn in the townhomes. The road was empty and lonely. James walked down the center of it.

The temple was at the end of the road. And just like Ryan had said, wooden planks surrounded the outside perimeter, and glossy, shiny, wet, dirt-brown concrete sat just inside. James's mouth almost watered at the sight of it. He sulked closer, hearing what Ryan said over and over. *It's rude. It's rude.* James tried to convince himself, too, but honestly James just thought it was funny. *Maybe I'll leave the penises out of it.* But he would make a story out of it yet.

James rolled his trousers up and carefully stepped over the board. His toes squished into the cold, slimy ground. He smiled wide. Then he leaned down very carefully and put a finger into the wet concrete next to his big toe. A sixth toe. Another dainty step, another added toe. Again. And again. He made his way all the way into the temple, where he shed his shirt, wiped his feet and the floor and admired his work. It glimmered in the moonlight. His smile widened.

Except, James realized, he hadn't figured out how he was going to get out of the temple. Then again, improvising seemed to be his strong suit. James knew no one would believe he *didn't* do it if the villagers found him in the temple the next morning. So carefully, James climbed out of the front door of the temple and scaled the monolith stones that made up the outside of the steep temple. His fingers hurt by the time he reached the roof. He wrung his hands, shook them out, then leapt into the nearest tree branch that overhung the temple. He admired his clever work one more time from a bird's-eye view then scuttled down the tree, shedding some bark in his haste.

James slept well that night.

When the morning came, the village surrounded the temple and the strange footprints. James came out from his townhome rubbing his eyes and yawning. *It's too early,* he thought.

Benjamin and Ryan were waiting for him, arms crossed.

"*What?*" James snapped.

"You did this," Ryan said.

"Of course I did it, but don't tell *them*." James walked up to see what the townspeople looked at. Murmurs and whispers surrounded him. When he reached the edge of the wood, six-toed feet gazed lovingly back at him. His finest work. James gasped for effect. "I've heard stories of this," James said. He looked at the people right around him.

They stared back, eager-eyed and entranced.

"These are the tracks of the Six-Toed Gnome," James said. "He's said to bring good luck to all those who see him and everything he touches. And it looks like he went into our temple. Surely that'll bring us good luck from the gods!"

A couple people nodded.

A couple people called his bullshit.

But James didn't care. He launched into a story about the Six-Toed Gnome named a painfully *normal* name: Owen. Benjamin and Ryan listened—despite knowing the true origin of the sixth toe—and the rest of the town did, too. That was how James became his town's storyteller. His stories had a ripple effect, too, causing confusion and chaos all throughout time to our very day, today.

bookseller

I hold the key to a thousand different worlds.

The Impostor of Hollow Ridge

Madeleine starts every morning the same. She has an hourglass figure, so she dresses to flatter. Waist-high slacks. A simple blouse. Madeleine likes to make an understated statement, so she keeps a collection of jewelry—inexpensive but vast—to make it. Today she chooses a peony flower pin. She straightens her long, black hair. She puts on her favorite wedge boots. Draw the cat-eye. Slip on the prescription glasses. Paint the lips rose-petal pink.

She gives her husband, Falkner, a multitude of kisses before she leaves their abode. Their life is simple, and Madeleine loves it. Falkner is a dream husband—the man who checked every mark on her boyfriend wishlist at age nineteen—and more. It started as a hoax; she read it in some tabloid magazine. *Make a list,* they said. *The universe is listening,* they said. Madeleine doesn't believe in "the universe," but she does believe in God, and she thanks God for Falkner every day. He is her godsend, and they make their home in a cozy one-bed, one-bath loft that always has sheet metal and drills in odd places; stacks of paper and newspapers and plates. They work hard for what they have, and they cherish it.

Madeleine works a simple front desk office job to pay her dues. She takes calls, restocks fliers, checks inventory, sends emails, and answers follow-up emails, too. Madeleine doesn't mind her job. The office is fine, with gray-stained wood walls that show all the imperfections of the wood. She likes that about the office she works in. All is not perfect, but her team works as a team, and that gets the work done.

The trouble starts when the intern makes her first appearance.

The intern—Marcelina—is a loud woman with a high voice and even higher heels to make up for her below-average height. Marcelina did not yet have a job at Madeleine's office, but she sure acts like she does. She wears huge sunglasses atop her blond hair, and she terrifies Madeleine like all other blondes do, too. She has wide eyes that search for any imperfections—the ones that Madeleine often thinks are quaint—in order to try to fix things that don't need fixing. And Marcelina's eyes fall on Madeleine first thing when she walks in. A mix of horror and what might be slight fascination crosses her face.

"Good morning," Marcelina says loudly.

"Good morning," Madeleine says softly. Madeleine isn't quite sure what she did to deserve the look so she smiles and goes back to her business. Checks her emails. Writes some reminders to herself.

But Marcelina is still looking. "We haven't met before," Marcelina says. *Way to state the obvious*, Madeleine is thinking as Marcelina extends her hand. "I'm Marcelina. I'm the intern."

"I'm Madeleine," Madeleine says. "I know." Madeleine has been expecting Marcelina for some time now, dreading it really, though she didn't let it show. She doesn't take Marcelina's hand; she has a thing about germs, and Marcelina smells like diapers and baby powder.

"I like your pin," Marcelina says. "Where did you get it?"

"The clothing store on the corner," Madeleine says.

"You shop there?" Marcelina has a look of distaste on her face.

Madeleine doesn't know what to think.

"Well." Marcelina lifts her brows and shakes her head. That's all she says. Marcelina smiles sourly at Madeleine before brushing past her and through the *Employees Only* door. Maybe to get her paperwork and meet with the boss? Madeleine doesn't know.

That night over dinner—frozen pizza, seltzer water, box wine, and Netflix—Madeleine tells Falkner all about it. "I feel like she hates me," she says.

"She hates you because you're young and beautiful," Falkner says.

"And tall," Madeleine notes absently.

"And tall," Falkner agrees.

Everyone loves Madeleine's long legs. Madeleine loves them too. She wears stilettos that night to bed to show them off even more. That night, Falkner especially loves her long legs.

On Tuesday, Marcelina's sunglasses are gone, and her hair is dyed black. Dark eyebrows are drawn on her face. She's two inches taller. Platform heels. "Good morning," Marcelina says.

"Good morning," Madeleine says. Madeleine thinks about her own long legs and the previous night. She smiles, and the thoughts slowly pull her away from what is happening in the front office and back to sheets slipping off the bed and the smell of Falkner's hair and the freckles on his shoulders.

"I like your pin," Marcelina says again today.

"Thank you," Madeleine says. It's a cat pin made up of a body of pearl and a head of cubic zirconia.

"I'm more of a dog person myself," Marcelina says. "Do you have a boyfriend?"

Madeleine isn't quite sure why that matters and wishes Marcelina would've asked something else of her; she loves Falkner but her value isn't defined by her relationship status. Madeleine thinks she brings a lot to the table on her own. Falkner complements her, and that's why it works. They complement each other. "Husband," she says simply.

"My hubby and I have been together for three years now," Marcelina tells Madeleine. "Kinda getting into that slump, you know? We're always looking for something to spice up the relationship. You know?" She laughs, high and shrill.

Madeleine *doesn't* know actually. She and Falkner have a fine relationship, and even two and a half years in, they still can't keep their hands off each other. They are madly in love, the kind of couple other couples envy. So Madeleine just smiles politely at Marcelina.

Marcelina leaves her phone on Madeleine's desk and says she'll be right back. She goes through the *Employees Only* door again. After a couple of hours—which *should* have been front-desk training—Madeleine finds out the hard way that Marcelina's phone is almost as annoying as Marcelina herself. Its ringtone is loud and infuriating. Texts on texts. Stacks of notifications keep the screen lit up. Madeleine likes to keep her phone on mute and her notifications on for her favorite contacts only. She even has apps on her phone to help mindfulness, to take her away from the noise, to focus on the real, the moment, the good.

That night Madeleine sleeps in Falkner's arms, thankful for the quiet.

Wednesday starts like it always does. Waist-high slacks. A simple blouse. Madeleine picks out an ocean wave pin and matching blue earrings. She straightens her long hair. She puts on her favorite wedge boots. Draw the cat-eye. Slip on the glasses. Paint the lips rose-petal pink.

At the office, she notices that Marcelina is already there. In fact, Marcelina is sitting in Madeleine's chair. Marcelina sits in her chair with straightened hair and eight-inch-high shoes beside her. Madeleine tries to brush it off, puts her stuff down beside where Marcelina sits with her feet crossed up on the office chair. (Her feet smell *really* bad, and it takes Madeleine back to her high school days when the popular mean girls flipped their stinky heels in and out of their shoes like an undercover mating call. Madeleine wonders if it ever worked for any of them.)

"Your birthday's coming up," Marcelina says without looking at Madeleine.

"It is," Madeleine says. She doesn't ask how Marcelina stumbled across that information. Perhaps one of her coworkers mentioned it in passing. Or perhaps Marcelina checked her personnel file.

"Do you have cats?" Marcelina asks.

Madeleine says yes. "Just one."

"I'm thinking about getting a cat. It would be nice for our baby to grow up with a friend."

"Why not a dog?" Madeleine asks. Marcelina had said she was more of a dog person, after all.

"Just thought I'd try something different," Marcelina says.

Marcelina leaves Madeleine's desk, and Madeleine works the rest of the day, shaken. Madeleine can hear it in her own voice, see the hesitance in her hand when she picks up phone calls. It seems Marcelina didn't like her much, so why would she care when her birthday was? Why bother getting a cat if one is a dog person?

"We're having a dinner party at *The Blue Diver*. Do you want to come along? I invited the whole team as an icebreaker." That is the first thing Marcelina says to Madeleine on Thursday morning.

Madeleine politely accepts, happy to hear some sort of offer from the intern. Maybe she isn't hated after all. The day flies by, and Madeleine gets home with butterflies in her stomach. It is her first invitation to any sort of work party; she is excited. She likes her co-workers a lot. They are a second family to her. To see Marcelina attempting to extend an offer like this is good, she tells herself.

Madeleine changes into something more casual. Waist-high jeans and sneakers and an oversized, gray cardigan. Falkner congratulates her, offers to drop her off. At the door of *The Blue Diver,* they kiss and Falkner wishes her good luck and a good time.

Madeleine gets out of the car into the cold, damp night. Lights string up and down and all around *The Blue Diver.* Cheery voices sound on the second-floor balcony. A live band strums a country song in the outdoor seating area. She walks up the few steps to the front door and slips inside. She approaches the server and tells him about her party reservation.

"Sorry, we don't have that reservation on the books."

Madeleine's hands grow cold. "They said it was *here,* at *this* time."

"Sorry, maybe they rescheduled it?" the server offers.

Madeleine leaves, confused. On the front step, she dials Falkner. "Are you close? Can you turn around?"

"Of course. What happened?"

Madeleine falls apart as soon as she slides back into Falkner's low-sitting economy car. She spills her story to Falkner over tears and staggering words. Did Marcelina do it to humiliate her? Why did she even offer? Was it the wrong place? Was it all in her head? The slow drive home and the smell of oil and metal and gasoline lull her to sleep. Falkner carries her inside.

Friday morning is chilly, and the tip of Madeleine's nose is cold by the time she opens the front door to the office. She finds Marcelina there, again, sitting at her desk.

Marcelina stands, walks around the desk, and offers a bottle of blood-red wine. She wears waist-high skinny jeans, sneakers, and an oversized, gray cardigan. Prescription glasses hold back her long, black, straight hair. "Happy birthday! It's today, right? I heard it's your twenty-first. I thought you could celebrate."

Madeleine doesn't take the wine from Marcelina's hand. Madeleine doesn't ask about dinner, either. She works her day, numb and cold, wondering if the bare trees outside are kinder than the intern. When she leaves that night, she reluctantly puts the red wine in her bag and locks the door behind her.

At home, Madeleine sets the wine bottle on their kitchen table then sinks into the old homely, teal couch in the corner. Falkner sits beside her, making a divot from his weight. He smells like hot oil and toasty bread and other spices she can't put her finger on. Tonight is supposed to be their date night, a night they cooked together. Madeleine had taken the long way home and arrived late, and now she feels bad.

"What's wrong?" Falkner asks.

"Everything," Madeleine whispers. She tells Falkner about her day.

"Let's drink the wine. At least then maybe the night will end better," he says.

They drink the wine together.

Marcelina starts her morning. She has a killer figure, so she dresses to turn heads. Waist-high slacks. A simple blouse with a cat pin from the clothing store on the corner. Draw the cat-eye. Slip on the prescription glasses. Paint the lips rose-petal pink. Today is her first day working a front desk position at her new office; they had a vacancy in the position. On her drive to work, the radio drones: *Two found dead in loft outside of Hollow Ridge.*

Drama &
the Muse

(Act II)

The Muse asked of Drama,
> *Why do you torture me?*

> *When you can have any of these other women?*
> *I am not nosy; I do not try to make friends or enemies,*
> *but simply fade into the background.*

Drama said to the Muse,
> *It is because I hate you.*

> *I hate that you are taller than me. I hate that you*
> *are younger and more beautiful. It's these petty reasons,*
> *our own insecurities.*
> *You are too good to fade into the background.*

fever

with sleep like splintered glass,
	fragile horror
		and misfitting pain;

my skin is licked with invisible flame.

I burn myself, with
fingertips of ice and
		numb steps;

		I can't rest.

I love you like the stars
love the sky....

I love you like the stars love the sky
wrapped in navy tourmaline;

I'm at home in your eyes
their evergreen wild;
    The sunset never looked so pretty
        as it did reflecting
        the gold of your iris.

My cells are on fire when we touch
electric (in your arms), burning to explode;
In all the vastness of your quiet,
your harmony, (your vibrant mind),
                I have room to grow.

I have space to burn ever brighter
        to be even wilder
        and uncontrolled.

You are an anchor that keeps me steady
grounded, but never run down
while I'm lost in the sky,
        drifting an atmosphere
of somewhere not unlike here.

If I live in two worlds, you're the one
who makes this one more fun,
more perfect, more complete;
You are the reason I believe
God made someone for everyone,
and I'm so glad you're with me.

memories in pink

Rose tinted glasses are just
        another word for love.

        A purple haze sky
that never dulls your green eyes.

So many memories of you
are painted this way—
        without outside views,
without vices so many others use.

We're in our own color profile,
one incompatible with
        opinions or rules.
                What the world says
                is not what our rule book says.

        Their shades of red
are of violence and revenge.

Our shade of red is the lipstick,
        the scarf I wore,
on our Valentine's date.
When others said, "He won't notice,"
        the first thing you said
                was, "You look great."

Their shades of blue
are calloused and bruised,
damaged goods.

But not with you.

Our shade of blue
is the forget-me-nots on my shoulders
                    and the roses on your suit.
                    My nails are crystalline,
                            just like your tie.

Their shades of gold
are of something old, something lost
an empire long gone…

But our shade of gold is the hazel
on the outside ring of my eyes,
                    molten fire in sunlight.

Just like your green, it never fades.

                            You fare my

winter soul

                            with roots in my

heart.
The veins in your hand,
            patterns I know
like the veins in my own.

My memories with you are pink.
Unlike all the others,
there is a filter on my brain

                    when I think of you.

You are safety, wine-red, maroon,
a deep mist of periwinkle and rose.

When I am with you
I forget about time,
I forget about my losses,
the trivial things I used to mourn.

With you

                    all of my
                    memories
                    are in pink.

30 Miles

I stand at the top of the bridge. A damp breeze whips through my untrimmed hair, smelling sweet and musky like lumber and undergrowth, like wildflowers and the ocean. It's quiet besides the wind; there is a storm front on the horizon. I think of what I need to do.

The storm will be strong, as they always are in the South during this time of year. Winds will be high; lightning will be frequent. I'll need to find shelter to stay out of the rain, maybe unpack my blanket and hunker down for the rest of the day. Evening is already close.

The dormant power lines sway eerily above me. There is no buzzing, no crackle, no low hum of electricity. There is no light in the distance to the north, west, or south. All the major cities are dark. I used to wonder what it would be like, before it happened. *What if the world was quiet? What if everything went dark?* Now I know.

It has its perks. The birdsong is more noticeable; the stars light up the night as they must've a thousand years ago. There is no white noise, no chaos. The chaos stopped right around the time the gas ran dry and the store shelves were purged of canned food and ammo. That was months ago.

It's funny, I think to myself. Years ago, a friend had called me a doomsday prepper as a joke. I'd never really thought of myself as that until the joke was made, and then the thought never left. I suppose it's true in a lot of ways. I've rationed my food appropriately, laid low. I have a hideout where I keep my stocks, tucked away in a discrete tree line, somewhere no one looks. The only thing I don't have is *him.*

That's why I'm out here in plain sight, risking the elements, risking being spotted and followed. As things were turning south on the political scene, he and I made a promise to one another: If anything happens, we would try to radio each other. Same time, every evening. From where I stand, I can see the two peaks of the tallest bridge in the city south of me. It's close to him.

I turn my radio on.

It's early. His alarm is going off. I pull an eye open and read the orange numbers on his digital clock across the room. Five-thirty A.M. Groaning, I poke him in his armpit until he squirms and rolls out of bed to shut it off. Immediately, I regret it. His body was so warm, I realize in hindsight, his skin so soft. I roll into the sunken center of his bed and watch him dress. Cute freckles dot his shoulders and back; it's a shame they have to be covered.

"I'm gonna grab some breakfast. Do you want a piece of peanut butter toast?" he asks.

"No," I say. I sleep until he tells me he's got to leave for work. It's a chore to locate my discarded clothes from the night before with my eyes as gooey as they are. This is my least favorite part of the day, too— leaving. We've been dating for a while now but haven't pulled the trigger on moving in. The distance is an issue. His job is here, his family is here. Thirty miles from where my job is, from where my family is.

When I'm dressed and packed, I gaze up into his face.

He smiles sweetly back. His hair is still a mess, pushed up and tangled on the side he slept on. There's a hickey on his neck, right above his collarbone. I almost pull him back into bed; I want to give him more. But he kisses me gently on the forehead and says he's going to be late if he doesn't go soon. His eyes twinkle, a promise to return to me in the night—either by text or by car. He'll be there. He promises.

We walk out together. The air is cool and slightly wet. The breeze is refreshing from his otherwise stuffy, dark room. Sunlight kisses my skin warm; he kisses my mouth the same. Fingertips brush the back of my neck. His breath is sweet and familiar on my tongue. We hug, tight, and it feels as if my heart is full in that moment. I'm no longer just half; with him I am whole.

I feel the distance—when I slip into my car, when I reverse and drive away, when I see him driving the opposite direction in my rearview mirror. On the way home, I see that bridge rise in the distance as I approach it.

The sun is just starting to rise, too.

There is no reply on the radio. I try not to let it make my stomach sick. I don't win that battle.

The walk home gets colder and colder. My leather boots are past *broken-in* now; the salt residue is beginning to wear away at the hide. I make a mental note to look for leather polish in one of the abandoned stores, but it's not high on the priority list. What *is* is a deep swig from my bottle of black spiced rum.

It's hard not to wonder: *Did he make it? Did something happen to him? Did he meet someone else, or all this time, was he just tired of me anyway? Was the apocalypse a good reason to part ways?* Surely not, I tell myself. Surely what we had was special. It *felt* that way, felt young and genuine and fun. Maybe that kind of thing just wasn't made to last the apocalypse.

My bicycle is at the foot of the bridge. My radio—still hopeful—is in my hand. Slowly, I shrug my backpack off my shoulder and put the radio away. I mount my bike, and as I do, a breeze whips through my hair. It's at least five degrees cooler than the last. The storm is nearing.

My bike creaks as I pedal; one of the chains rattles. I've done my best to maintain it in the months following the fallout. It was one of the first raids I did—a cycling store. I took a few cans of WD-40, spare chains, and the only spare tire ring they had in stock for my tire size. Those rations are about halfway gone as biking is my main method of travel.

I remember loving biking before everything went dark. It was easily one of my favorite pastimes. It was one of *his* favorite pastimes too, something we bonded over. It's hard not to think about that as I ride home.

✻

"I know a place. It's at the preserve. They have good mountain bike trails," he says.

I am wary, as the most intense biking I've ever done was to the highest point of the island and back—which isn't that high. But I agree, ever wanting to be the ideal companion. I'd heard that's what men wanted—someone who can keep up with them, someone who can be a workout partner, someone to have adventures with. In the past, I'd filled that role among my coworkers at the hands-on rental company where I worked, quickly earning a stale reputation among their wives and girlfriends. Few women ever seem to like me. I don't seek attention from men either; it's just something that happens naturally. With him, it's harder. I find myself aching for his attention, pulling at every string I'd woven flawlessly in encounters past, hoping I can still show the careless, confident persona that drew so much unwanted attention before.

This is different.

Even though I have a headache, I push through. I drink water sparsely on the mile ride to the preserve, worried I'll have to pee and dreading the choice of either Porta-Potty or bush. When we get there, it's beautiful. The parking lot is all gravel and stone, the gates in front of the trails are all wood. Everything is natural, untouched by the corrupted world around it.

I don't feel the wind in the trees as we bike. He bikes ahead of me. (I tell him to so I don't slow him down. I promise him I'll catch up, tell him to enjoy himself.) Little flecks of dirt from his tire sting my eyes so I put my sunglasses on. It keeps my contacts from drying out, too. We dodge fallen and hanging limbs, and spider webs that are ornately weaved between low-lying branches. When we stop for water, mosquitoes land on us. The feather-light touch is concerning—an ever-present threat of a week of irritation—so we move quickly.

The trails are more intense than anything I've biked before. The hills burn my thighs, my lungs. The descent is pure adrenaline. I hold the cool, metal hand brake, worried I might slip and tumble into the ravines at the bottom of those fast-paced hills.

Leaves crumble beneath our tires; branches swish high above us.

I don't know where he's headed, but I trust him, and finally we come out to a clearing. We bike over some loose rock out among the marshland to a man-made dock that's two flights up. It stands higher than the low marshes around it, a square pillar lookout to admire the landscape around it.

He takes two steps at a time.

I take deep gulps of water before struggling up the same wooden stairs. The air smells like salt and fish, like humidity and wet wood. The sky above us is a dusty blue, and in the distance, there is a billowing storm front that races nearer. We're on borrowed time.

Together, we inspect all the drawings left before us on the wooden, weather-worn railing—an extremely detailed eye drawn in Sharpie, a jagged lightning bolt, "Tommy was here," initials of lovers (V+R, C+C, J+S). We leave our initials with my pocketknife. He kisses my damp forehead, brushes the sweaty tendrils of my hair behind my ears. The first specks of rain poke at our skin. It's a relief to me, a change from the burn. But he doesn't seem so happy about being caught in the rain.

I don't mind it. I never have. The rain is always a relief for me. It's a break from the sun, and it always seems as if it's come to wash away all the burdens and weariness of days past. *Rain* and *rest* are synonymous to me. That doesn't change as drops of rainwater begin trailing down my face. It's light rain, and the shoulders of my shirt are the only part that clings to my skin. My backpack is barely wet by the time I arrive at my tree line.

I flip my kickstand out and approach the shrubbery. Used to be, I had to pace from a chip in the road—exactly fifteen paces—to find the fake branches I'd placed in front of the entrance to my hideout. Now, as if it's muscle memory, I just know. I drop the branches down, roll my bicycle through, then lift the branches back up behind me.

The road before me winds deep into the woods. It's all dirt, the mailbox long knocked awry by a storm and left to rot. The house on this property was abandoned after everything went dark. I'd scoped it for weeks before claiming it. Luckily, there was no major damage to the structure, the wood, roof, or any other vital part.

I begin the walk towards the property. The tree cover only allows sparse droplets of rain through, though they are bigger than they would be without the leaves they slide across and combine on. They leave big, wet kisses where they fall. I roll my bike in through the front door—as I've done every night since—hoping that this would slow the deterioration and rust. I shed my backpack by the door, too. I wander to the kitchen—where my rations are—and bring down the rum from the top shelf. Usually, the quiet doesn't bother me; usually, it's welcomed, like an old friend. Tonight, the quiet and the patter of the rain outside is the sound of loneliness and despair.

It reminds me of the quiet that we had together, but in a hurtful, nostalgic way. Our silence was comfortable, familiar. We could sit together in his room and watch a movie without talking; we could eat at a restaurant and only need to speak with our eyes. His silence complimented mine.

We sit together in his car. We're driving the city highways at night. Orange lights flash overhead, man-made stars twinkle in the distance. We're silent. I mention this.

"It's not a bad thing," I follow it up with. "It's a good thing. It's like," I pause, "I can feel your frequency." I feel silly after I say it. "I

know it sounds superstitious, or whatever, but I'm not really like that. I mean it like… Well, I can just feel *it."*

"I think I get it," he says. The pulsing light illuminates the lock of hair that falls over his nose, the thin patch in his beard which is still growing in at twenty-seven.

"I guess the best way to say it is…" A breath. "At my job, right? When I work with the guys. It's quiet then, too, but each of them feel different. One of them, the silence—the frequency—is like a compliment. Like we know the same things about life, yet none of that needs to be spoken. The other, it's like the silence of a sibling. And everything is just right. Conversation is easy because we both exist in the same frequency, or one that compliments. Like two notes on a piano," I add. "Harmony."

"I get it," he says. Not in a just-stop-talking sort of way, but a genuinely thoughtful kind of way. "It makes sense."

To myself, I think, it's the first time a man has taken me seriously for my outlandish nonsense, my sixth-sense sort of intuition. Though, I can't say I tried it with anyone else.

I go on. "Some people, when you're around them, their frequency just rubs you the wrong way. Makes your hair stand on end. Triggers your fight or flight instincts." I don't elaborate more on this, though it's a feeling that I'm all too familiar with. Family and friends—I'd known a handful of people who grated silence with their energy, made it something charred and crooked.

But this wasn't like that.

I lean my head back on the passenger seat, listen to the whir of the pale interstate below his tires, and gaze at him.

He gives me a swift smile in return, flashes his sideways canine at me.

In the silence of my lonely house, I think this: What if he was just tolerating me? What if I was out of my mind to even voice that at all to him? What if he was waiting for the right time to cut me loose?

Rum bottle in hand, I untwist the cap and take a swig straight from the bottle. The dark liquor burns all the way down, opening my nasal cavity and pricking tears at the edges of my eyes.

Outside, the rain begins.

I sigh and sink into the leather armchair in the living room. I gaze out the windows, watch the rain dance across the river's surface. Palm trees shudder in the wind. Tomorrow, I leave. Tonight, I memorize every corner and crevice of this house. Tonight, I say goodbye.

I drift to sleep thinking of the nights we sat together at his desk—with me on his lap and his arms circled around me to reach his computer—and the virtual adventures we had there. I dream of a digital world where we walk through different doorways together, each a new level, a new palette of colors, a new soundtrack, a new objective, a new phase of life.

The rain is a thrum of white noise on the roof when I wake. My eyes are gooey, stuck together. I don't bother checking the time; in the end, it doesn't matter. My bag is already packed and all there is left to do is *leave*. There's one stop I have to make before I head south, one that will benefit my trip.

I have one plastic-wrapped raincoat left in the kitchen drawer. I kept it just for this trip. It's green—a color I have always associated with him. I told myself, as I tell myself now, that I will find him. I cannot give up hope; I cannot give in to the voice of doubt that eats at the edges of my mind. So I set those thoughts aside.

Everything I might need and what little I brought to this house when I first arrived is already in my bag. I packed my first aid kit, the MREs I bought off a coworker before things went south, my journal that I keep in a plastic bag, two extra water bottles filled with water, and a cleansing tablet. I roll my extra, dry change of clothes up and stuff them in the top. I dress in something more waterproof—Columbia shorts and a wind jacket beneath the raincoat. Last to go on is my pair of leather, waterproof boots.

The house is still around me, and I take one more glance around it. It's served me well in the weeks I've spent here—been a quiet, dry place to shelter. In its own way, it had quirks. The memories would've been more potent, more precious, had they been shared with someone I love, someone like *him*.

I whisper a goodbye to the house nonetheless before I close its door for the last time.

The tire of my bike creaks slowly, tiredly, as I make my way down the path back to the main road. I know the journey ahead will be long, so I do my best to fortify my mind, to let my energy lay low inside of me and agree to hold out. The air is damp this morning with leftover humidity. I anticipate my stops already: the first will be to El, the second will be this evening, and then I will go from there.

El isn't hard to find. She never is.

It's the edge of summer. We take our bikes and drive to the island. I know the best spot, I told him, and he listened. Now here we are, unloading our bikes at the edge of the Greenway. We spritz ourselves with bug spray, then lock the car doors.

It's the perfect day for a bike ride. The sun dips in and out of clouds. The breeze threads gentle fingers through my hair. We pedal side by side on the matted grass path. At first, we're silent, in wonder of the nature around us. It's not that the island isn't full of life everywhere else, but rather, this is the part of it that's untouched, the artery of wilderness that pumps life into the rest of the land here. Storks bend gracefully at the water's edge, reed-like legs still as can be. Bunny rabbits dash across our path, close enough to make us both jump and giggle. We spy turtles sunbathing in the creeks alongside us, peel our eyes for baby gators—or mama gators for that matter—but see none.

Then we talk. It's a natural kind of conversation, something sweet and humble, about beginnings. Where did we begin? Would we have ever stayed in touch if I didn't kiss you the way I did? That sideways kiss that was meant for your cheek? You turned just in time to make it funny—to make it a half-lipped kiss. I apologized, asked to try again. We both laugh at the memory.

"Have you ever gone to an apple orchard?" I ask him.

He thinks. "Maybe once," he says.

"Back home, we had an apple orchard that would have a fall festival every October," I say. "They had the best apple cider, all sorts of activities, big tents where people could sell things like balloon animals and handmade candles. The best part was that you could get on a hayride to pick your own pumpkin. They had a corn maze, too! Every year they made a different design then hung pictures of all the designs by the cash register inside their store."

"That's cool," he says. His voice thrums through me, calming any jitters I might've had.

"Have you ever been through a corn maze?"

"No," he says.

I explain that our mazes always had trivia that I thought was pretty silly to help guide us through left and right turns; I wanted to be challenged by a maze, not hand-held through it. He says the only thing he really knows about corn mazes is a horror movie where someone is being possessed and chasing the others through the maze. I say I hate how predictable horror movie endings are, and he says he understands with a laugh.

In the distance, a storm is blowing in.

The change chills my skin.

"At the end of the trail, there's an ice cream shop," I tell him.

He looks over with windblown hair and eyes as evergreen as the world around him.

By the time I make my way up to the small, covered area, the rain is just a patter on the plastic on my skin. The area is sparsely populated—but more so than other areas on the island—with few other dwellers giving me sideways looks. This part of the island has come together as a community; it's a nice change from what I've seen elsewhere.

When El spots me, she jumps off the picnic table and walks up to me. Her dark skin is pallid in the hazy weather, her hair a tangled tuft of grown-out pink. Without hesitation, she launches into me, and I return her hug, grateful for the now foreign feeling. Before it happened, we used to scour this beach for sharks' teeth and shells together right as the tide went out. Now, I can only guess at what she's been up to.

"Oh my god, *areyouokay?*" The words tumble from El's mouth.

I nod, forcing a small smile. "Good as I can be."

She searches my face. "What are you doing here?" A wary question, something she might have guessed at, something I'm second guessing, myself.

But the truth of it: "I was wondering if you could help me… If you could tell me how safe it is, south of here." I pause. "I'm trying to make it into the city."

A smile spreads across El's face. "Lucky for you, we've had people pass us traveling north. I think I may have some information for you. Come sit for a while," she said. She leads me over to the covered picnic benches. All around it, tents have been set up. Campers park around the outskirts of the lot. It looks like a small city, and I have no doubt these people have used some of the empty homes here to their benefit, too.

I flip the kickstand on my bike and set it in the sandy grass right outside the covering. When I look up, El is standing before me with a freshly cracked coconut. "Here," she offers.

"Thank you," I say.

We both sit, and I lean against the table, taking this precious moment to let my guard down and relax. I realize now, as I sit here, that I have been completely unable to do that simple thing: *relax*. How could I? Even my nights, what little fitful sleep I get, are light and on edge.

I close my eyes and breathe deep. All around me, I feel and hear the familiar—the damp, salty air on my clammy skin, the distant swell and crash of the waves on shore. Hearing conversation drift in and out is a new but welcome sound; it's been too long without hearing other humans talk.

El lifts a plastic box onto the picnic table; when she sets it down, glass *clacks* around inside. Her first raid was a beauty shop. She told me over the radio, on one of the first weekends we spoke after the panic. She told me the goal was to trade information over manicures. I told her it sounded crazy but that I loved it nonetheless. In the end, it worked. I watch as El pulls out a few different colors. She lets me pick the color, and I pick green—the same green as *his* eyes.

El smiles knowingly. She met him, in our past life.

The memory comes back like a ray of sunlight after the wind blows the clouds away. I'm sitting on my bed, before I met him. I'm doing my best to focus on the small book in my hands. The cover is slick and soft at the same time; the shades of steel blue on the cover are some of my favorites.

I picked up the book because I'd read the author's first book and enjoyed it. Though, this one is about love—something I've sworn off. It's been years since my last relationship, and in the meantime, I decided I would stay single to focus on myself, to heal and love myself. It's a break I needed, but the book in my hand has the door to opportunity cracked again.

I read the chapter, skepticism still lingering in my periphery, the color red bleeding away from my sight—as if the book has opened my eyes to a new view of men—one where they're not all sexist scumbags. In this chapter, the author talks about how she made a list of all the things she wanted in her future husband. She writes she had no reservations while writing the list. She put every single thing she wanted.

Ridiculous, *I think.*

Sighing, I pick up my phone and pull out my notes list.

Funny, cracks jokes, makes people laugh
Sweet, smiles a lot
Self confident and knows worth
Ambitious
Understanding
Pretty, light-colored eyes
Cool with tattoos
Has good relationship with family
Loves God
Apolitical
Would go to a shooting range for a date
Good at conversation
Great jawline
Sporty
Loves road trips
Likes to read/appreciates art
Tall/fit/lean

I leave number eighteen blank. I give up. I put my phone away and keep reading. Outside my bedroom window, the sun is setting over the lake in my backyard. The water is still as glass, and it reflects a sky full of cotton-candy pinks, blues, and purples. The clouds dot the horizon, and I think I spot a small, fuchsia, heart-shaped cloud.

I stay the night with El and her community in order to rest up for the remainder of my journey. In the morning, we say our goodbyes. I hope to see her again soon, but in times like this, it's always hard to know if that will happen or not. We agree to radio each other the following week to catch up.

The salty water that crashes off the ocean just over the dunes burns my eyes as El and I give each other one last hug.

"This isn't goodbye," she says. "It's just *see you later.*"

I smile through the tightness in my throat.

It kills me to tear my eyes away from her. Part of me wonders if forces outside of our control will make this our last meeting. I try to push those feelings down as I swing a leg over my bike and steer back towards the main road. *Don't look back. It makes goodbyes harder.* I close my eyes for a moment instead, until I exit the parking lot and make it back onto the road. With my eyes open, I try to commit the road to memory—the live oaks that sway above me, leaves rustling, and the green growing all throughout their branches, trunks, and roots.

Cool wind whips through my hair as I take a deep breath. It smells of salt and pine and the sea. Mentally, I brace myself for the road ahead. I don't expect to see many people out on the road, but perhaps, others will be hiding in the state parks along the way. I'll need to be on guard, just in case.

The first thirty minutes fly by. I hit a bridge that overlooks the end of the river that divides the island from the mainland—one of the two ways off the island. The view is beautiful. Waves break all along the beaches that line either side of the river, creating white caps that look like lacy frills on the edge of a beautiful blue dress. In the distance, off to my right, two men are fishing over another dilapidated bridge. They don't turn to look at me; all for the better. I can't imagine running into a stranger on my trip.

The bridge lets me off onto a new island. The first few moments are adorned with beautiful bays of nature on either side. White storks and great blue herons glide across the sky overhead. I even spot a bald eagle swooping into the tree line.

I pass a state park on the left and gaze in longingly. Our second date had been there.

I sit in my car and pull at my hair nervously. Mirror down. I check my teeth, my breath, the light makeup I put on. I pat my pockets and make sure I have everything I could need.

My coworkers had joked endlessly that I'd agreed to meet him at Boneyard Beach. Dirty jokes and be-careful-you-don't-end-up-as-a-pile-of-bones jokes, too. I tried my best to put that out of mind. I've already met him, and he doesn't seem the type. But that's what they all say. The killers are always the ones you least expect.

His car rumbles past mine in my rearview mirror. Gravel crunches under his tires. My stomach somersaults inside me. I glance at his car. He's checking his mirror, his chin lifted just ever so slightly. Spotty scruff covers his sharp jawline. My stomach flutters again. I pat all my pockets one more time—damn the nervous habit—then get out of the car.

He meets me halfway.

He's so tall that I have to tilt my head to gaze up into his eyes. They match the forest—green with flecks of gold and amber. He smiles, kisses me.

His mouth tastes like earth and salt, and we dissolve into our surroundings. For a moment, I am nothing more than nature itself—in abandon in the kiss, lips moving, breath stirring, fingertips on my neck, and a hand on my back. It feels natural, the way that it's supposed to. I am meant to be with him, and he is meant to be with me—like summer storms that rage above the sea.

We smile at each other after the kiss, an unspoken acknowledgment that he feels it too.

Hand in hand, we make for the tree line and the trail I know that hides there, which leads out to the beach. As we walk, we talk about the little things in life that we might've otherwise not shared: where we went to school, our favorite subjects to learn about, who our best friends were, and the trouble we got into when we were young. This is the baseline for a relationship, the finer details that give you a rounded view of who you're looking at. I find that I'm looking at a boy who let his friends pick him, who fought his way tooth and nail through his studies.

The trail lets out on a steep, sandy hill that leads to the beach. We stumble down the shifting sands and make our way to the water. It's almost still, lapping at the sand quietly. I could listen to that sound forever. We walk along the tide line as the golden evening sun stretches between the trees and across the packed sand of the beach. We find ourselves at a small river that splits the beach, and we stop.

I turn to him.

He's golden in the sunlight. Green eyes gleam.

I ask him about the fundamentals of a relationship—about where we stand with politics and basic rights and how we feel about family and starting families of our own. Every answer he gives aligns with mine.

The road before me is longer than I could've ever anticipated. The trees all begin to look the same. I take a break after a few hours to drink some water and eat one of my MRE packs. The food is dry and crumbly and sticks to odd places in my mouth. I try to swish a sparse amount of water around my mouth so it'll last me the rest of the trip. I don't know how long I can keep this up—traveling on the road with limited supplies. It was never going to be a long-term thing, but even knowing I still have another full day ahead of me is exhausting to think about. I try to set a pace that's sustainable, but I can already feel my strength waning.

The storm from before has long passed, but the air is still sticky and heavy with humidity. My clothes cling to my skin. I shed my rain jacket and tie it around my bike handles. The air isn't cool, but it isn't too warm either. With my movement and speed on the bike, the breeze is able to keep me cool enough, but the further the sun gets into the sky, the warmer it gets. Sweat trickles down the nape of my neck; I can smell a faint waft of body odor coming from myself. Though, I guess that's to be expected. I make a mental note to make a stop at the beach sometime soon after my trip. I've always found salt water to be effective for a lot of things—including sweat.

It hits me all of a sudden—how much I miss how it used to be before things went dark. I miss my day trips to the ocean to swim. I miss the feeling of saltwater on my skin. I miss the late nights I used to go to the neighborhood pool with *him*.

Those nights float back to me in hazy delirium from the heat. As the evening fades, I fade back into my memories.

Summer nights in Florida are something else. They're hard to capture with words because they contain multitudes of sensations all wrapped around you at once—the dark sky and the fiery stars that shine in masses that you cannot see close to the cities, the humidity that towels your skin slick with sweat. Summer nights in Florida are the sounds of cicadas, of frogs, of a fire snapping from your neighbor burning a pile of brush that the latest hurricane stripped from the trees and bushes and deposited across lawns and driveways. It's the way the moonlight reflects off puddles of summer rain on hot, black pavement. It's the smell of salt water from the proximity to the ocean; the smell of chlorine and plastic, flip-flop sandals.

We run to the neighborhood pool in fits of playful laughter and screeches. We stumble through the gate, leave our meager belongings on the white-and-black metal and mesh pool chairs.

He runs and jumps into the water—the motion-activated lights casting a calm orange glow over the illuminated pool. Electric teal water ripples around the dark mass of him before he surfaces. He shakes like a dog—sending water flying in all directions.

Cool droplets prick my skin, though I'm several feet away from him and the pool. I slip off my shoes and make my way over to the water. I go for the steps, not ready to fully commit like him. My feet touch the pool water, and instantly, nerves and muscles unwind all over my body—as if I've just been coiled inside a massive rope that's just gone slack and fallen limp around my ankles. I go deeper; submerge myself to my neck. I keep a careful eye on him as I dip my head back—careful to wet my hair and not my face. I'd be damned if I messed up the makeup I worked so hard on for him to appreciate.

He swims closer.

Water trails down the side of my face then spirals into my ear, causing chills to form on the back of my neck.

His green eyes gleam like smoky quartz in the low light. His hands curl around my bare back in the water around us.

All our movements are effortless and easy. I let my body float against his as he carries us mindlessly around the pool. We talk about the future this time—about where we want to set down roots, where we want our careers to go, what we dream of in a house, and if we can even dare to dream like that at all. It feels like the world has stacked the odds against us; even moving in together poses a bigger challenge than either of us expected.

Rules. There are so many rules for us. Make three times the rent. Have a job for three years. Don't have pets. Don't do this; don't do that. We read the pool rules for kicks: Don't drink and swim. Don't swim after ten o'clock. Don't run around the pool area. Don't jump into the pool.

He and I look at our water bottles—which have been filled with wine and beer—and then to the moon that's high in the sky and then to each other and laugh.

"Fuck the rules," he says.

"Fuck the rules," I agree.

I guess now I have no more rules to worry about. At least that's the upside of everything going on.

My journey is nearing an end, and all I can think of is the downside.

I'm standing on the top of a bridge. This time, it's the very bridge I scouted the day I planned to set out on this journey.

My breath is fire in my lungs. I can't seem to get enough. My ears popped a couple of times on the way up, and now all I can wrap my mind around is trying to *breathe*. I step off my bike and lean it against the side of the bridge wall. I put my hands on the wall, too.

Over the edge, the water looks like rolling fabric below me. It's so far down that I can't make out the tiny white caps individually, only that they look like piling on a well-loved sweater. I close my eyes. Breathe in. Breathe out.

Wind whips around me, tugging at loose strands of hair and caressing my sweaty face. I wish I could just stop here. It's the first time I've considered giving up. It was hard enough to get to the top of this bridge—I don't anticipate crossing it again. Either I commit and go down—towards him—or I bail and go back the way I came.

I try my radio one more time.

Still, no answer.

Just static.

My nerves turn static, too.

The night is cool this high up.

And I have a decision to make.

I look back over the edge of the bridge at the water again. It thrashes and breaks in chaotic patterns—ones that cannot be predicted by man. I wonder for a moment how it would feel to go swimming in such a wild body of water. It's something *he* would do. Hell, it's probably something I would've done in a past life, too.

Now, as exhaustion laces every inch of my body, I can't imagine being tossed about by the waters below. All I want is to rest in his arms for the next week. I want to sleep with no concern for tomorrow. I want things to be the way they were before. *I want things to be the way they were before.*

Maybe they will be.

I have to hold onto that hope.

Once I've steadied my breathing, I mount my bike and stare down the massive bridge. It'll be a coast all the way down, and I'm ready for it. I can use a bit more of a break.

I take one more breath then push off.

The tires of my bike roll of their own accord.

The wind picks up.

My stomach pitches with the decline and the steady pace that my speed picks up. I knew from the beginning of this journey that *this* would be the most challenging part. Now, as my bicycle hurdles itself down the steep road, I find myself relieved that the hardest part is over. I feel more and more at ease with every passing second, with every inch I get closer to the approaching exit I'll take.

As the bridge levels out below me, I begin to pedal again.

Just ahead of me, I see a sign. On it, my lucky number. I say a silent prayer that that means something now—just like it did *before*. Can my luck hold out a little longer?

The night closes in around me again.

The road is a mess. I white-knuckle the steering wheel; my eyes, though dry, stay wide open. I keep an eye on the thermostat in my car. Thirty-four degrees. The temperature has been dropping over the last thirty minutes of my drive. I knew it was risky, being on the road this late, but I couldn't help it. I need to see him.

We agreed to meet at my place tonight. He got off late; I got carried away catching up with a friend at the shopping center. My place was the agreed-upon place to meet—mostly because of the forecast. He would stay the night; we both have the next day off. But his *place didn't have the same forecast.*

Snow—in Florida.

With my hands steady on the wheel, I fight the nerves by focusing on the giddiness. I've lived here for years and heard legends of snow—the snowstorm in 1989 specifically—and always secretly hoped I'd witness the phenomenon myself.

Now, there's a real chance.

The temperature reads thirty-three degrees.

Rain hammers against my windshield, making the wet pavement shine eerily and camouflaging any worn-down lane lines. Every so often I have to squint to make sure I'm still where I should be on the road. There's only so much more of this I can take, *I think to myself. I turn on my radio, pick a neon album with a spray-painted black smiley face on the cover. The familiar bass and beats rumble through my car speakers, sending tremors up my spine. It calms me, if only but a little. Makes it easier to focus. I fall into a trance—autopilot.*

The album takes me back to summer, to late nights sneaking into the pool and kisses on blankets at the beach.

My mind swirls like the rain outside.

If I can just make it back before midnight, I'll beat the freeze.

I keep my eyes on the thermostat, begging it not to drop to thirty-two.

By some miracle—and the gas pedal floored to eighty-five miles per hour—I make it off the interstate and onto the exit that takes me home. I slow at the red light, thinking of that word. Home. *Is this place home? Or is it him that makes it home? Or is it both?*

Green.

I pull onto the main drag through town.

The rain on my windshield sounds sharp now, clicking against the glass. It's brighter in my headlights, more reflective.

It's ice, *my brain tells me. I've seen it before, up north, before I moved. It looks like stars speeding past a spaceship, a reminiscent call back to my childhood and innocent years. Now, it doesn't feel so innocent. It feels* dangerous.

I'm drained by the time I get back. I cut the engine and sit quietly for a moment.

Hail pitters against my windshield and sunroof. Ice slides across the surface and accumulates on the corners of my windshield. I stare in awe.

In the parking spot beside me, he sits in his car, waiting. He looks at me, eyes aglow with the same wonder I feel. I get out of the car and he meets me there. I open my hands to the ice falling from the sky, only to notice that it's getting lighter and lighter—but not in precipitation. In weight. The ice is turning to snow.

The moment hangs between magical and surreal as snowflakes drift silently through the early morning. I do everything I can to commit it to memory, to place that feeling in a secret compartment in my heart and hold it there forever.

We make mini snowmen on the top of his car until our hands are bitter with the biting cold and our clothes are wet with snowball fight hits. We run into my apartment together, our laughter billowing in puffs of steam in the cold air. We make a fire to warm ourselves up, though it takes well over a half hour for me to regain feeling in the tips of my fingers.

The night is perfect, and exhaustion claims me quickly as we lie side-by-side in my bed. Golden-orange light is cast across the ceiling, and quiet snaps and pops lull me to sleep.

In the morning, when I wake, he's not in the bed beside me.

The final stretch of the journey has my stomach somersaulting inside of me. I begin to notice more and more people as I go. It comes as little surprise; the closer I get to the city, the more it's to be expected. Most are on foot, huddled in small groups, eying me warily. I return the favor and pedal faster.

It shouldn't take more than another hour or so to make it to his place. The Florida wind brushes through my tacky hair. I want more than anything to take a hot shower, but I know, even if I make it safely, that won't be an option. At best, we might be able to make a trip to the beach to go swimming. I think about the last time we went—how the water on the south end of the island was unusually clear. The bright teal still lingers in my mind along with the piercing yellow sun and the way it livened his eyes. His eyes: they're painted so clearly in my mind. I can still see the thick clumps of his dark lashes and the red around the rims of his waterline from the salt that stings him there. His irises narrow then widen, flexing the olive-and-moss green within. The waves dipped and bowed all around us, and in my mind, we remain suspended there.

Heat rolls in waves off of the concrete below me. Sweat pours down my temples and my back.

Soon.

I have to keep reminding myself.

I'm almost there.

I'll get to feel his arms around me again, his chin on the top of my head. *Soon.*

I can't wait to *smell* him again. The thought almost makes me laugh out loud. I can't help but wonder if he might be in the same sort of predicament that I am—smelly from not showering. I'm sure it won't be the same pine-and-citrus cologne I remember so well.

I follow my internal compass through each abandoned street light. Store parking lots are empty. Restaurant windows are dark and vacant. It's a ghost town in the worst way— because there are no bodies left behind and there are few people to be spotted. It makes me wonder where exactly everyone went. Closer to the heart of the city? Traveling like me to find their way to allies, friends, or family?

My stomach twists violently again. I'm acutely aware of my radio bouncing at my side.

Why didn't he pick up?

The first thought is slow, but it undermines the foundation I've so carefully laid. An avalanche follows.

What if I came all this way, and he's not here? What if I came all this way, and he wants nothing to do with me? What if the whole time he was just leading me on? I'll look desperate. I'll look needy.

I stop myself to listen to a much quieter, much softer voice.

You'll look committed. You'll look like you care.

You'll look strong.

Then another thought hits me, sinking my stomach like rocks in my pockets.

What if he came looking for me, and I missed him? What if, in my search for him, we passed each other unknowingly? Could we ever find each other again after that, endlessly cycling back and forth, hoping that some miracle will find us stranded on the beach where we carved our initials on a downed tree?

What if I never see him again with no explanation?

What if when I get there, he's gone and the house is empty?

What if I never get a response on my radio?

What if I never see his smile again?

What if I never see his eyes again?

What if I never hear his voice, never get to call his name and watch him light up when he turns to face me?

The worst goodbyes are the ones that are never explained.

I turn right onto the road that leads to his neighborhood. My memories pass me one at a time like ghosts: when he drifted us in his car at the light in the pouring rain, when we took our bikes off-road while the sidewalk concrete was being poured, when we biked miles out to the preserve, when we raced back to his place—trying to beat an oncoming storm.

Humidity threatens the back of my throat, making it hard to breathe.

I remember hosing down in his side yard to cool off, how it felt for the sweat to wash away, how he kissed me after with cold lips and a soggy tee.

I turn into his neighborhood.

Focus, I tell myself. I remember each conversation we had in his car at each stop sign, at each turn.

"Do you want to go see this band in concert? I got free tickets."
His eyebrows raise, mischief glitters in his emerald eyes. "Yeah!"

The lump in my throat refuses to budge; the pit in my stomach is intimidating enough that I understand. I feel trapped in a loop of memories, our old haunts, and the way he was everything I ever dreamed. Lifetimes swirl around me, making my vision blur at the edges.

All I want is him. I want to be in his strong arms. I want to taste his lips. I want to fall asleep to the strong rhythm of his heart. I want to count the freckles on his shoulders while I wait for him to wake up. *There is nothing I want more.*

I turn onto his road.

It's downhill, and I coast.

His place comes into view.

I don't even hit the brakes before I jump from my bike and run across the yard. Grass crunches softly under my boots. My backpack *thumps* against my spine. My heart thunders inside of me.

I make it to the door—the vacant concrete block that's a dead giveaway that *no woman lives here*, the familiar pattern of dirt daubers' nests that spot the stucco. The creaky glass door.

My heart beats in my throat.

The door opens on its own.

I'm finally ready
to write a poem
about you

They say there is a fine line
between   love and hate;
                           fear and rage.

I hate how you make me feel
everything at once.
Am I not enough?

I'm finally ready to write a poem about you
because you made me cry
for the   second time
                    tonight.

The first time was fine.
They were happy tears
—with whom I'm well acquainted—
shed always by myself
never with some*body*

I hate that it was you
I shared those tears with—
because now it's *you*.
It'll always be *you* who I loved
                    first.

I love all of you:
your pimples, too;
ingrown hairs and your ticks and tells;
the way you rub your fingers when
                    you don't want to share
or you're uncomfortable with the truth.

But *I don't want to share*

                    —ever—
the way you nod your head when
                         you're happy;
when we're together in bed when
words just don't quite say what
          you need them to
          say; the way you think
          with wandering eyes
and find your resolution in mine with

                              a swift kiss.

                    It's bliss
                    to be with you.

Your evergreen eyes and the crystal skies
make me feel the same
                    wonder as a child.

                    How can you be mine?

But tonight I wonder:
Are you really even mine?
Am I enough?
Or am I just something you come (in)to
                                        so you're not alone?

I was fine alone.

You said it was nice to have a girlfriend.
I think it's nice to have you.
                        But mind-reading was easy
                        until I met you.

Now I don't know if you really love me,
or if I just fall too fast—
with my heartbeat in my cheeks,
        I swore to myself
        you were worth risking ruin,

        but that ruin
        would be worse than death.

alexandrite

You can find the different sides
of my personality—my true colors—
under three different lights:
aquamarine green by photography,
wine red by candlelight,
and London topaz blue with you.

The Lil Lagoon

It was justa normal Saturday afternoon when the No Good Northerners, Miss Bean and Little Bean, sat in their backyard watchin' the lil lagoon a their property. Their house sat a shy ten feet ta the lagoon, so they always had ta keep an eye on dem gators that liked to sunbathe in their backyard.

All a the sudden, Little Bean noticed a lil party across the pond.

"Must be the people who just moved in."

"They're fishing," Little Bean said.

The lil group a boys skirted a house over, right on the ledge a the lake. They went on yappin' loudly, crackin' open sodas, an' tossin' trash left and right on their path 'round.

Miss Bean and Little Bean watched 'til the boys were just one house over—right at the line a their own backyard! Miss Bean didn't think she needed ta explain how small their backyard was and how close the strangers would be ta her own bedroom window. Not ta mention dem gators who frequented the spot. If Miss Bean gave dem boys permission ta be on her property and somethin' happened ta dem, it'd be on her homeowner's insurance. And Miss Bean was a No Good Northerner who knew common sense rules like that. "You can't be here. This is private property," Miss Bean told the lil delinquent, knowing they wouldn't understand the bigger picture.

"Well mah mamma told me I can fish right here at the edge!"

"You can't be here."

The boy argued again, "I can fish here!"

"No you can't."

The boys finally left, but not before Miss Bean got a good ole picture and posted it on the good ole in'rnet. She captioned it: "Parents should tell their children to stay off private property. We need to discuss this matter as a community."

The homeowners filed out onto the street, one by one, ready 'n eager for the drama ta unfold.

"Ya know you should be grateful they ain't vandalizin' your property!" Mama and Papa Weeksley shouted. They had wide smiles and neckbeards.

Little Bean thought that sounded a lot like a threat. "Comparing one wrong to another doesn't make it right," Little Bean said.

Rick Wadsworth stepped up next—a *very* short man with a *very* big truck. "They was just enjoyin' the great outdoors! What kind a babies can't take it if some good, God-fearin' young men be out der fishin' the pond?"

"I was just trying to encourage parents to teach their kids to do the right thing," Miss Bean said. She didn't think the Southerners around her could comprehend anything about insurance and liability. So she just went with the obvious, "They were trespassing."

"Nuh uh!" Wadsworth waved a small, meaty finger. "There be an easement there—between your property and the lake! That's common space!"

Little Bean watched as a couple other narrow-minded Chads rationalized why it should be okay for some teenage boys ta be loiterin' around back behind the Beans' house. After all, an easement only allowed the *easement* holder ta be there—and dem boys weren't even sure what an easement really was, no less *who* the easement holder was like Miss Bean did!

"Well if it were my house, y'all'd've been welcome!" one said. And another, "Those good, lil God-fearin' boys can come fish in my backyard anytime!"

"Thank you for your kindness."

"Nah, ma'am thank *you* for *your* kindness."

"No, sir, it was on this good ole God-fearin' woman ta be a good example. Fishin' is fishin' and it ain't hurtin' nobody."

The good, upstandin' White Men of the South nodded solemnly.

The No Good Northerners thought it was kinda funny, so they did the upstandin' thing ta do in the South, cracked open some beers, and laughed it off.

Justa 'bout five minutes later, there was a hammerin' on the door. Instead of wavin' through the window and closin' the curtain on the uninvited guest (like Little Bean knew was best), good ole Miss Bean opened the door.

"Hi," the woman said. "I'm Kelly Bragger." She had spikey blonde hair—the kind all done up and streaked with the bleach highlights tryin' ta look all normal and all that. She put her hands on her hips—feet wide—ready to take on the two No Good Northerners inside. "How dare you blast my parentin' skills in front of the whole damn neighborhood like that!" She waved her hands around as if she were famous! *Don't you know who I am?* she seemed ta ask as she stood there— trespassin'—on the Beans' property.

"Trespassing is trespassing. I own this property."

"Why didn't ya just ask dem who dem parents were?" she spat through two missing front teeth. Or, shoulda been missin'. She had two, big ole blackened cavities in the front a her teeth from talkin' all sorts a fake sweet stuff in her life, the good, God-fearin' Southern belle. "If ya didn't know who dem parents were, ya should'a asked dem boys! They woulda told ya!"

"I was a camp counselor once—" Miss Bean tried to explain the time she looked after kids at a music camp—ya know the good ole time when she asked a disobedient lil boy who his camp counselor was but he wouldn't tell her—but Kelly Bragger wouldn't hear it.

"I never been ta counsellin' in my life!"

Little Bean snorted in spite a holdin' back a laugh.

"And I'm dun with your smirks!"

Little Bean burst into laughter.

"Ya know what! Ya won't have ta worry 'bout my boys on your prop'rty again! No wonder our fees went up! It's all 'cause a negative people like y'all drivin' other homeowners out!"

"Get off my property!" Miss Bean yelled. She waved a hand in good riddance.

"Call the cops!" Kelly yelled as she paraded her double-wide, rhinestoned behind back out to her car. "Call the damn cops!" Louder, for the ones in the back. Ya know, dem gators, which if her good, God-fearin' boys had been eaten by dem gators back on that "common space easement" behind the Beans' house—it woulda been private property. *Her* property, goddammit! Miss Bean's! But that wasn't the song bein' sung on that good ole, sunny Southern day.

pain & flowers

most days I feel that my body has betrayed me

it's falling apart. my ribs slant sideways, and
my spine likes to sway;
my scoliosis lays claim to the credit
for my hourglass figure,
                my chronic pain

I read somewhere that 'they say' that
if one who has chronic pain
        —voices their pain—
it means that the pain is unbearable
and at twenty-four, no one believes me

but who are they to say what my body
                is
        and what it is not?
my body is a blessing and a curse

my beauty betrays me too. it cheats
me out of credit I should have had:
        for hard work, for hard labor, for a
        creative mind and wonderful fables;
        for the stories I thread and weave out
        of the nothingness of space;
the stories that I sow myself into,
my masterpieces. but I am nothing
more than the pretty face

I am more than the pretty face and
this body that deceives me

I am worlds within worlds;
                    I am a creator
I am limitless, beyond this sack of flesh and bones,
this debilitating pain and this gross figure

even if my joints dislocate, my disks
slip, even if my jaw has a slight crook
that no one notices—
        the one that makes it so hard to sing the songs
                    I love so—
        I would still create

because when I write, when I draw, and when I
reap the harvests of the relationships I grow,
                    I feel free
I have been unlocked from this crooked cage, the
        world of pain
the two anchors of my feet that tie me to the ground
            and I can fly
            when I write
I ease the pain when I draw,
and I feel the flowers that bloom on my skin
through the crevices of broken concrete bones
            when I lay with the one I love

because even if my body betrays me,
    it also creates me
it makes me into a creator;
it is my temporary home,
and it is sacred. it is my own.

roses

I planted roses on the day you turned me down,
    dirt between my fingers,
    bruises on my knees.

I needed to feel the love in the labor;
needed something to speak to,
    something I could please.

They say plants grow better
when you whisper kind words of affirmation
into their leaves.
Brush your lips on their petals

        fingertips
        on thorns,
        velvet green.

I can see why they flourish,
because I feel like I'm losing my mind.
I can see why they bloom carelessly.

I've been spending all my time
tailoring my petals
to be the right shade of pink;
the pretty blush on my cheeks, which
you don't always think

                      twice—
I'm hiding the bags under my eyes
    from restless nights

of spending my days, pulling fingers
                    painting nails
                    biting skin
to get the words just right,
because if they're just quite right
you might just like
what I have to say—

the story I have to tell.

It's not an easy one;
It's never been.
It's never been harder
to say what's on my mind.

Because I'm covering my face,
picking the colors of my dresses
to be something to appeal to the masses.
            I've tried to conform;
tried to make the truth—that painful truth—
    an easier dose of medicine.

And I've overdosed myself, too.
I've forgotten how to bloom.
Because all this facade has left
is a shell of your "best luck."

The day you turned me down, I realized
that I've become a waiting game—
        waiting to be watered,
        waiting for the rain,
        waiting for the sun to tell me
                it's my time to shine.

But so high up in the sky,
how can you know what it's like?
To become a shell, to become a game,
to become a pawn used
          for the queen
          or the king
          or the rook?

You took it all from me, the day you turned me down,
so I told myself,
          I won't let *me* down.

The Giant in the Hardware Store

Only women work at the hardware store. It is such a well-known fact, in fact, that the hardware store is actually called *The Chix Fix*.

Every now and then a stranger will pass by town, needing a hammer or a drill or a piece of wood. The stranger will walk into the store—smell plywood, feel that solid-smooth concrete beneath their feet, gaze up into the high-hung rafters—and think: *This is what a man calls home.* The stranger will be alarmed to find that only women work there. Subtle at first, he might seek out help from someone else. Maybe not so subtle and a tinge chauvinistic, he will leave. (This never happens with women, of course, as a woman lucky enough to find a hardware store run by women would never frequent another.)

Say a stranger—a man—does accept the staff. He will soon notice that none of these women stand higher than five feet. Not one is five-one. Not five-two. All four-ten or four-eleven. They all have long, long hair so glossy that it moves like a spill of oil on their shoulders, maybe curling like a river-worn root, or graceful like smooth white clouds on a breezy day. They all wear pointy shoes, too, which is something any tall-standing man would notice fairly quickly when he looks down on these curious women.

Today's stranger warily approaches a small woman who is organizing a shelf. He is very aware of his steps, as if he's scared he might frighten or startle her. She has the same complexion as a deer—with fair brown hair and two, puffy white earrings that almost look like earmuffs on her small (slightly pointed) ears. She wears a plain, wood-brown dress that reminds the stranger vaguely of a coffee shop and dark brown, pointy, wooden shoes. They clack as she turns to look at him.

"Hello there," the small woman says. She has freckles and wide eyes.

"Hello," the stranger says. He reads her tag. Her name is Amber. He thinks he might tell her his name is Ossian, but he doesn't. People don't usually tell each other their names at a hardware store. "I'm looking for the multi-tools. I'm here on a trip—left mine at home."

"This way," Amber says. She clacks away.

Ossian takes a moment before he follows. As he follows Amber, he looks down the tall rows and feels sort of as if he's lost in a forest. The racks are all a burgundy-wood color and the lighting up in the rafters is a soft gold. He swears he sees them flicker every now and then, blink at him like creatures or fireflies. He shakes his head. But the women in the aisles are just as strange. They look like bunnies or foxes or even sometimes like toads. A couple blinks makes a normal-looking hardware store return to him. He's being silly, he tells himself.

Amber stops at an endcap. "Here," she says.

"Thank you," Ossian says. He takes one multi-tool off the rack. He checks out and leaves the store in a slight daze. The sunlight on his face feels cold, and he suddenly realizes the hardware store had been surprisingly warm, like a secret oasis in a desert. He glances back as the glass door slides closed.

Amber is looking at the glass door, too. She sees that look on his face and adds it to a growing list of expressions that men who've accepted help at *The Chix Fix* have had leaving, as the stranger just did. The women who come through never have that look; they come in and leave smiling and in their next visit their smiles are always bigger, as if the hardware store is a nail salon or hair salon or retail therapy.

Amber recalls, as she walks to the back of the store, one man who asked for management. He was a tall, cold man with eyes like icepicks who stood with a severe curve in his back.

"Management is busy," Amber had said. The man left shortly after.

Management is always busy, but management is also always conveniently unavailable. That is the best-kept secret at *The Chix Fix* and it kept a lot of drama away. No one wants to argue with short, agreeable women, so the strangers tend to leave. And the short agreeable women are often very, very competent in what they do. The only thing they can't do is reach the top shelves.

Amber's next customer came in needing just that.

Amber's next customer is not a stranger or a man. She is a middle-aged woman with wrinkly brown skin and short gray hair and a sparkling smile and eyes like chestnuts. This store is better than shoe shopping for her. Her name is Nakoma, and she loves this hardware store. She loves Amber, too, and she reminds Amber of all this on every one of her visits.

"My dear, I need another box of flooring. The special kind. Top shelf." Nakoma winks.

Amber smiles. "Let's put in the order."

In the very back of the store—that's where the owner's office is. That's where the husband and wife team hide themselves in fear of instilling fear in their ever-loyal customers. Though, in reality, it is the wife who is the owner of *The Chix Fix;* her husband is the one everyone loves, who cooks goodies—pumpkin spice cookies during fall; peppermint bark during winter—who keeps the friendly front when his wife has to make hard decisions.

Dalia is the wife. She is tall (obviously) and spindly in her own way. Her arms are cords of muscle, tawny and spattered with greenish-brown freckles. Her hair is a pale, reflective blond, the color of sand in the sun, and her eyes are all blue.

She is slow when she moves, deliberate. She is a craftswoman above all else; her strength comes second.

Syon is the husband. He is shorter than Dalia, but only just so. His hair grows like moss on his head, close and trim, and his full beard lays in braids over his thick chest. But despite his overall stockiness, Syon's attention to detail never lacks. He cooks his treats masterfully and true to size. He cooks much like an adult using a child-sized kitchen, crouched over and slaving for the finer details.

That's what they do now—sit together in a low-ceiling room in the back of the warehouse. They sit close, back to back. Dalia can feel the faint heat from the small kitchenette, and Syon can feel the brush of Dalia's wispy hair. The sweet smell of sugar cookies waft through the close air. Dalia enjoys it. Syon hums pleasantly.

Amber enters the office. "Dalia," Amber says. "We need some boxes pulled from the top shelf."

Dalia nods; she is a gentle woman of few words and complete with a golden-retriever-loyal heart. Dalia follows Amber out of the cramped office and into the flooring department. She breathes in the smell of laminate and stone, of hardwood and dust. Though she loves it here—though her store is as close to her heart as it can possibly be—it is not home. Home *was* here, years ago, but not long ago. Dalia misses it dearly. Sometimes, when she picks up a box or a panel example of hardwood floor, she will feel the echo of the Forest's heartbeat, a dwindling patter, much like the ruffle of wings as a flock of crows take flight.

The soul of the Forest is still here, though fleeting.

She feels it now, which perhaps can be to blame for her falter, for her temporary lapse of present-mindedness. For even though the store is now closed, she does not notice the human's eyes until after he notices her. He is a timid type, one that reminds Dalia of the dryads who used to live in the Forest with her.

The next day, the sun is hazy in the sky, shy and wary. It's as if all her secrets have been spilled before her, the safety of the town and its long-buried heart at risk. The sun would've set right back down on the horizon if it were up to her, just to keep time from moving forward.

But that's not what happens.

What happens is this.

Ossian wakes in his hotel bed, drenched in a cold sweat. He has barely slept. In what fragmented time he has, he dreamed wild things. Dreams of eyes bigger than his hands, blinking at him from over too-tall shelves. Dreams of unusually small women with pointy ears and pointier shoes. He dreams, too—to his own alarm—of a deer-like woman named Amber.

And when the sun tickles his bare toes, he realizes with a violent shiver that none of these things are dreams.

Yesterday, Ossian entered a hardware store full of dwarves and giants.

Today, Ossian isn't sure what to believe. He'd returned to the store after hours in hopes of acquiring Amber's number, but after seeing the giant, he'd run from the building. He hadn't stopped running until a peculiar man with a round nose and autumn-orange hair standing outside a pizza shop had shouted at him. Then, Ossian bent over, hands on his knees, and panted until he caught his breath.

"Sir!" the man said. "Are you okay, sir?"

Ossian nodded.

"Water, sir?"

Ossian nodded again. He sat on the wooden bench outside the pizza shop and gasped a little more.

The orange-haired man returned with a cup of water and a personal pan pizza in a to-go box. "You look like you need it, sir. For good luck."

Ossian accepted the gift and walked the rest of the way back to his hotel.

The hotel entrance slid open, and a round man with dark hair and a red face welcomed him flamboyantly. "Welcome to the Forest Inn!" For a moment, the man struck Ossian to be some sort of animatronic fortune teller, something you might see at a circus that springs to life at any motion.

Ossian had thought it was simply that the man who worked there truly loved his job. It wasn't until the host asked him what three things might make his night better that Ossian questioned it. Those three requests—a bath that smelled of lavender, cashmere pajamas, and warm blankets—magically appeared in his hotel room upon his return.

Ossian is still in his new cashmere pajamas. "He is a genie," Ossian concludes aloud, just to make sure he hasn't yet bargained away some essential part of himself—his voice, his sanity, or otherwise. "And the pizza man is a leprechaun."

Ossian considers his sanity may already be gone.

It is the sharp pain and hollow ache in his stomach that finally pulls Ossian from his hotel room. He dreads the idea, knowing once he leaves his room he will be subject to all the strange happenings outside his room in the Forest Inn. Room 104 has been a sanctuary of sorts, but it is not enchanted and all of Ossian's pizza from the night before is gone.

Ossian does not change out of his cashmere pajamas— they are a steady presence of comfort. He glances in the mirror but once. Reflected back is a mop of sand-brown hair and watery, glazed eyes. A few strands of hair stick to his forehead, where his skin is flushed and splotchy. Gone is the sight from yesterday—the adventure-seeking soul wayward-bound and heaven-bent on finding a new place to belong.

Ossian fixes homes for a living, and he has so far lived in a trailer mini-home he built with his own hands, pulls it with his modest, yet efficient truck. He was commissioned to fix a home for a mysterious woman with pale green eyes that often turned yellow in the sunlight. (Ossian tries not to wonder any further about that.) Across the street, the first afternoon he'd met his client, Ossian had noticed a house for sale. Ossian scheduled a walk-through that same day, found it was the home he'd always searched for.

But that was yesterday.

Today, Ossian wonders if his client is secretly a dragon. Today, Ossian wonders if he'll leave the town alive—or rather—if the town will let him leave at all.

Ossian pats down a few tufts of wily hair and breathes deep. He will try.

The door handle is cold on his fingertips; when he turns it, he finds himself greeted with a brush of cool, fresh air. His room is stuffy, he realizes. An afterthought. He steps out. The hall is vacant, though there are noises coming from the dining area—smells, too, the sweet batter of fresh waffles, bacon, orange juice, and muffins with sugary, crumbly tops.

Ossian's mouth waters. He ventures down the hall, towards the smells and sounds.

He is greeted with a sight he should have expected—the flamboyant hotel host (the genie), the orange-haired pizza man (the leprechaun), and the small woman from the hardware store (Amber). They all turn to look at him.

Ossian stops in his tracks.

When Amber makes eye contact with him, she holds his eyes there. Steady. She looks even less ordinary now—as if the Forest Inn has shed some light on a supernatural hue of her.

*

A fog lay heavy over the town. It stretches like the cotton insides of a child's teddy bear—thin and fluffy, clumpy in spots.

That is outside.

Inside the coffee shop, Amber and Ossian sit at a table together. The pizza man and hotel host sit at another table trying to look inconspicuous; they do not. It is obvious they are listening to the conversation that is now happening between Amber and Ossian.

A waitress sets two steaming white cups before Amber and Ossian. Her braids slip from her shoulders and twinkle as they knock against each other. From his periphery, Ossian thinks he sees snake eyes wink in the woman's hair, but when he looks, he only finds small golden beads wrapped around the woman's tight braids. She gives Ossian a dark smile then leaves the table.

Ossian twists the cup in his hand. The shop's logo is there in stone-gray: a woman within a circle, with circlets of snakes all around her face—coming from her hair. He swallows.

Amber takes a sip of her coffee. It smells as sweet as nectar as the steam blooms between them. "So," she says, "you saw my boss."

"I saw your boss," Ossian says hollowly.

"There is something you must know," she says.

"The pizza man is a leprechaun? The hotel host is a genie?"

"He's a djinn," Amber says.

Ossian glances at the other table.

Both strange men look away.

"This land is enchanted," Amber says. Her fingers curl against her cup, the tips of her nails a warm, earth-tone brown. "Was."

"Is," the hotel host mutters.

"Is," Amber says. She looks at the steam rising from her coffee, so much like the fog billowing outside.

Ossian wonders if he were to look for any fantastical shapes in the fog if he would indeed find them—or if they would simply be a figment of his imagination.

"Once, there was an enchanted forest here. There are many enchanted forests all over the world. Ours was sold, developed," Amber says. "We were left without a home. The only place to go was into the development. We could not save our Forest; they took no heed to our words."

"There is a way," the leprechaun said, standing suddenly from his adjacent table. "But simply getting her help will be a battle of its own."

Ossian and Amber turned to him.

"Do you want to come sit?" Amber says pointedly.

The men slink over, dragging loud metal chairs with them. When the four are situated, the leprechaun and the host sit.

"Introduce yourself to my friend," Amber tells the men with a newfound authority about her.

"I am Doug," the hotel host says.

"And I am Declan," the leprechaun says.

Ossian shakes both of their hands.

Declan jumps right to his explanation. "There is a woman who lives on the west side of town," he says. "She is named Ryoko. She used to terrorize our Forest, back when the trees grew tall here. She was a Sleeping Dragon." Declan's light eyes flicker across the table—to Amber, who drops hers, then to Doug, who nods solemnly. "Sleeping Dragons are notorious for setting fire to villages when they wake, once a fortnight. She destroyed our homes, over and over."

Ossian ponders this. He thinks, too, about the woman and her green and yellow eyes. He wonders if she could be the same. He thinks, if but for a moment, that the coffee that the woman served him is letting him see more about the world than he usually would, making connections that are there but not present, clear—yet not obvious. He looks to the counter where the young black woman brews a new pot of coffee. From between her braids, an oil-slick snake lifts its head and blinks at him with all-seeing eyes. "Where does Ryoko live?" Ossian asks.

Amber writes down Ryoko's address. "We've delivered some home-improvement equipment there a few times already this week," she whispers, ashamed. "We got it wrong the first time, so Dalia made us all memorize it. That's the only reason I know." Amber hands the paper to Ossian.

It's the address of the home he's been working on.

Ossian leaves the coffee shop with a sense of foreboding hanging over him. He realizes that he *is* much more aware of the world around him, that his barista is indeed the healer of the townsfolk, and that her special brew is said to open the drinker's Third Eye of Understanding.

Now, Ossian is seeing wolves made of white mist brush around his calves, doves swooping in the fog above his head. He walks to his hotel, knowing he will find his way. He does not worry, no. The barista's drink is said to have calming effects, too. Amber, Doug, and Declan only mentioned this on their way out when Ossian asked if they saw eyes in the mist.

He should be afraid, but he is not.

He *should* stop walking when a woman begins walking beside him, too, but he does not.

"I am the one you seek," she says.

Ossian glances at her, as if he is trapped in a trance. Of course, he spoke with her in passing, while working on her home. He always thought her to be elusive in the way a princess might be—well-mannered but reserved. Dainty. Careful. Meek (not to be confused with weak). Somehow, hearing what Declan had said made sense. He could imagine her as a dragon now, thin and lithe and powerful, with a tail like a razor blade and claws like pickaxes.

She has long hair made of black wisps that trail behind her in the hazy atmosphere. Her eyes are green, but they gleam with intrigue. "You know what I am."

"How did you find me?"

"I hear everything that happens in this Forest," she says with a voice like a river.

"They said you could help."

"I could," Ryoko says.

"Will you?" Ossian asks.

Ryoko lifts her chin, stares ahead into the haze of mist. "They told you I destroyed their homes," she says. "What they do not know—what *you* do not know—is that it was a mere misunder-standing."

"A misunderstanding?" Ossian wonders aloud. Setting whole villages on fire? Surely not.

"Declan means well." Ryoko stops walking.

The fog clears slightly. They stand before Declan's pizza joint, *Full of Goodness Pizzeria*. The store is closed, windows dark, but left outside the front door is a single chalkboard fold-out sign with this week's special. It reads, "Céad Mile Failte." The neon red light casts an eerie hue on the words and the dragon before him. Her human eyes turn on him, gleaming orange. She looks feral, looks like fire incarnate.

Ossian finally has enough sense to step back.

"Every two weeks when I would rouse—the first thing I would smell is his damned *pizza*. The bastard. He uses too many hot peppers in his signature dish—the *Hot & Saucy*.

Every time I woke, it would tickle my nose. It would make me *sneeze*," she sneered, teeth bared.

Ossian's jaw gapes. He can't believe what he is hearing. Surely he is mistaken.

Ryoko pauses, realization dawning on her face. "You don't know what happens when a dragon sneezes," she says slowly. Fury returns to her features. "Well," she says sharply. "We breathe fire."

"This could have all been stopped."

"Yes," Ryoko says. "But they never listened to me. All I wanted was to talk, but they feared me. And this idea they have—to save our Forest, it won't work without burning the whole town again. Would they allow that? Would they not see me as a villain again?"

"Maybe they would be open to it," Ossian offers. "Maybe if you spoke to them, talked to Declan about his peppers— maybe we could all reach a resolution." Ossian notices he says *we*.

Ryoko notices, too. "You are not one of us."

"No," Ossian says, "but I feel drawn to this place. I want to make it my home, too." He can't quite put a finger on why he is saying this to Ryoko. "I want to help."

Ossian sits in a cafe in the next town over. Clinks of silverware surround him. Mundane conversation fills his ears, a hum of everyday life—what's for dinner, what's on tonight, what's happening this weekend… Ossian sips his coffee while the TV drones in the corner. He pretends not to feel the smoke in his lungs, pretends not to care as he watches a fire rage on the screen.

"This morning, authorities were alerted to a wildfire blazing through Elwood. Despite the fire department's best efforts, nothing could be saved. The threat to the firefighters posed a larger risk, one man said, making it the safer option to evacuate the town and let the fire run its course."

If Ossian watches the screen closely, he can see figures moving about, a woman handing cups of enchanted coffee out, and a leprechaun holding a handful of chopped peppers close enough to the snout of a very large, very lethal silhouette. If he squints even harder, he swears he can see two giants lumbering around, moving the Enchanted to safety.

In his mind he hears Ryoko's words, *Clear up this confusion. Tell your friends I will help them. Then, leave this town. That is what you can do to help. When this is all over, you may return, so long as you help us bring our Forest back to life.*

All is right in the Forest.

Amber walks through the trees and shrubbery—all which sprout vivaciously from the help of the newly fertilized soil (thanks to Ryoko's fire) and the tender care of the garden gnomes (graciously led by Owen and his team of six-toed men). Amber ventures away from today's festivities—in which the Forest people have gathered around Declan's new circle pizza stove which was built with the help of Dalia and Syon. There is no drama today; Declan graciously vowed no peppers would be used without proper warning, and Ryoko has finally joined in on the Forest peoples' gatherings.

But today, Amber seeks the quiet, the stillness and serene of the Forest and its evergreen soul.

She delicately steps over new, sprite-sized twigs and blooming wildflowers. Deeper into the Forest she goes.

Scarce attempts to develop have been made since the first fire; every time, Ryoko has swooped in to the rescue, scorching the new buildings with violent, raging fires. She went from villain to savior, and Amber couldn't be more grateful. Their forest was safe, thanks to the dragon with a temper.

Amber stands in a small clearing and stares up towards the sun. It beams down on her. The trees whisper and laugh brightly around the edges of her vision; the wind brushes her hair from her neck and tickles her cheek. Finally, all is right.

A shuffle sounds across the clearing.

Amber looks.

She is stunned to find there something that she missed upon first stepping into the clearing: a small, yet efficient truck with a camper attached. Standing before it is Ossian. He holds one hand out as if he is trying to calm a wild animal.

"Ossian," she says his name in surprise.

"Amber," he whispers.

Amber runs to him and, uncharacteristically, leaps into his arms. With gratitude overflowing—for the man who convinced Ryoko to help restore the Forest, who played a part in bringing her home back to her.

"Wait," he says. "Look." He untangles from her, dashes back into his camper, and retrieves a paper. "I petitioned to preserve this land as *protected lands*. They approved it!"

Amber takes the page from Ossian's outstretched hand and reads it slowly. Sure enough, the paper is stamped with yesterday's date. No more construction; no more people; no more risk. Their Forest was finally safe, *truly* safe, thanks to a human man who stumbled into *The Chix Fix* nearly a year prior. *It took a small army,* Amber thinks to herself and smiles. "We should show the others."

"The others are here?"

"Of course," Amber says, smiling wider. "Follow me."

in sound

My neck is played by a horsehair bow,
    quivered with melodies high and low.

Each disk in my spine takes a beat,
    a rhythm that gallops together in
        percussion resonations.

My muscles to the tips of my fingers,
        the strings of a piano
        hammer with harmonies;
    and each rib hums in unison—a gentle bass
    that thrums through my bones.

My skin jumps each inclination,
    each half step
    and
    whole step
    as the song rises—

The decrescendo drops that symphony of sound
            into my body once again;
and the last note hangs my hair suspended,
        hovering my brain in ecstasy,

      in sound.

Sally & the Interview

Sally had to land a new job. She worked at a terribly dull office as a chiropractor and couldn't stand it. Something about touching people irked her; it wasn't really her idea to become one in the first place. It was her parents.

"It'll make good money," they said.

Sally didn't really care about the money. Sure, she needed to get by, but a pay cut and a dose of happiness would do just fine—might do the trick actually.

That was why she was outside at three A.M. under the speckled, starry sky and a harsh spotlight, scrubbing the pollen out of every crevice in her little, Neptune blue car. You see, Sally liked cars. Sally *really* liked cars, actually, so much so that she was going to absolutely nail her interview tomorrow— today. In a few hours. Seven o'clock sharp. She would drive her pearly car right up to the detailing shop, step out in boots and jeans and a ponytail and flash a grin as crystal as her clear windshield. She just had four hours to go.

As Sally saw it, her car was her resume. Those guys at the detail shop would be stunned—*deer in the headlights,* she thought cheerfully. She thought about cleaning deer guts out of the crevices of tire rims, and much to her surprise, it brought a swell of relief. She was finally over touching hairy backs and hairier toes and bending arms over heads and catching a deadly waft of BO. She was finally going to be happy.

In the pitch black of that moment just before dawn, Sally envisioned her future. She would defy the box she'd been placed in. No longer would she be her parents' prodigy of the "American Dream." No. She would make her *own* American Dream. She would work with the boys. Get dirty like the boys. Be *respected* by her coworkers and clients.

And as the sun began to lighten the sky to the periwinkle blue and lavender hues of dawn, she took in the sight of her love in life.

The poignant blue of her car was electric in the morning light. The highlights were cerulean and the deep shadows were a vibrant indigo. The red pinstripe slashed across the middle of her car, ready to race right to her interview.

She was ready. Or at least, her baby was. The carpet inside smelled of lemon and new fabric. Hanging from her rearview mirror, she'd placed the closest thing she had to lucky dice: a festival bead necklace made entirely of small, gold dice.

Sally checked her watch—a gift her ex had given her. It was a wheel that spun on its axis, a steady red break sitting right below ten o'clock and eleven o'clock. Sally liked the gift too much to get rid of it; most often, when asked where she got the gift, she just lied and said she bought it for herself— to match her ride—to save any awkward conversations.

It was six A.M. now, which gave Sally just enough time to shower and hit the road.

Inside her studio apartment, she did just that. She threw on a white, Indy 500 tee that had a hole in the left shoulder seam and tied her unruly red hair into a bun. She glanced at the mirror and briefly thought of covering her freckles with concealer. True, she was fond of them, but would the guys at the car shop think her too reckless? Too soul-eating or ginger or crazy?

Her alarm beeped on her wrist.

"*Shit*," she muttered. No time.

Sally grabbed her leather men's wallet and crammed it in the back of her paint-splattered jeans then dashed out the door. She hopped in her car and turned the ignition. Her car purred to life.

Sally turned the radio on, pulled up her confidence playlist. It would cycle *I Like It Heavy* by Halestorm, *World Class Fuck Up* by New Medicine, and *American Dream* by DIAMANTE and her other best headbangers the whole way to her interview.

Windows down. Sunroof open.

She was ready.

Her car whipped out of her parking spot. Hit the brakes once, then slung out of the parking lot. She made her way to the front of the neighborhood, just polite enough to keep the music down until she hit the open road. Then she cranked it.

Her radio sang sweet guitar riffs as the wind licked through the stray strands of her hair, coiling fingers around her neck, and raising goosebumps on her arm. This is where she felt most at home. On the road. On her own. In her car. Free.

She wanted to help others feel this way too— unrestrained, completely their own. She thought this was always best achieved when one loved her car. Because in Sally's mind driving a car and freedom were interchangeable, synonyms, completely the same.

Thinking of the interview was the last thing on Sally's mind. She put it *out* of mind, actually. She always did her best when she *was* her best. So she focused on that. Being her best, most authentic self. Being *wild*.

Finally, she thought, *finally, I won't have to be who my parents think I should be. Aren't I old enough to have a say? I'm going to be who I want to be.*

Sally pulled her car into the white-gravel lot of the car detailing shop. Stone crunched beneath her tires. All around her, there were cars. It was right out of a dream. Small silver racing cars. Suped-up, low-riding gangster cars with blacked-out windows. Cars with stunning paint jobs or striking racing stripes. Sally tried to steady the stampede in her chest. The little white paneled building was everything she dreamed up close. An awning stretched over the wooden porch and front steps. A calico cat sat on the railing; two green bowls sat side by side on the porch. She took a deep breath, stepped out, and closed her door.

Her car beeped as it locked.

This is it, she thought. *Good vibes only. Let's go.*

Sally recalled the email she received regarding her interview: *Go through the front door. The office will be the last office on the left. Knock, and we'll let you in.* She did just that.

The white door before her was silent.

Then, color flooded her vision.

A man stood there—a remarkable six-plus feet for Sally's remarkably short town. He had chestnut eyes and curly hair and gave off an overall vibe of an oversized teddy bear. He welcomed her in. Inside the office, there were two other men: a lanky one with a purple baseball cap and a short one with surfer-blond hair and tattooed arms.

The first man pulled out the chair before his desk and asked her to have a seat. "My name is Riley," he said. "These two are Ash and Adrian." The other men waved respectively. "Did you bring a resume?"

Sally's stomach dropped to the pit of her soul.

Riley waited.

"Sir, I didn't bring a resume, but I cleaned my car to show my skill," she blurted.

Riley nodded. He stood, a blue plastic clipboard in hand. "Let's see it."

Sally rose, her heart pattering yet again, and led Riley and Ash and Adrian out to her vehicle.

"Aw, I love these. My wife used to have one!" Adrian said of Sally's blue hatchback.

Sally unlocked the car.

Riley circled it, opened a couple doors, then inspected the wheels. He ran two fingers on the underside of the wheel well and inspected them; there was nothing but his own two fingerprints that came away. "You're hired," he said. "When can you start?"

"Tomorrow, sir," Sally said.

Riley opened his clipboard up and pulled out a white sheet of paper. "Now I'm gonna be honest, we can't keep work here for nothin' so…"

Riley held the paper before Sally. It was a W-4, gloriously blank.

She gazed at it.

"You've got the job if you want it."

She took the paper with shaking hands. The W-4 crinkled against her throbbing heart. "Thank you. I'll be here tomorrow."

"Great. We'll see you then. Seven o'clock sharp. Bring your finished paperwork with you," Riley said.

A grin split Sally's face. She did it. No more obscene hairy body parts would glare at her day after day. No more schmoozing up to her parents, or her parents patronizing her about things she detested. She was about to live her own best life. And as far as she could tell, these men would let her be herself.

They would let her be wild.

stars

One by one,
we took the stars from the sky

    to put on planes,
    on cities, and
    carvings on concrete.

One by one,
the stars in the sky stopped shining;
    their names, forgotten and
    their stories, ancient history.

One by one
they became
lore and legend,
and eventually,
        just lies.

The stars,
one by one
by one by one,
were robbed their promise
to govern the night sky.

One by one,
we took the stars from the sky.

But one by one,
    —when the world goes dark,
    the night the noise is silenced,
            and the lights burn out—

the stars will return to take back
the name given to them;
    the power to turn tides,
            to change seasons
            and to rule the night.

Death Meets the Child of God

otal darkness. That's what it's like the night of His birth.

You watched. You've watched for a long time, in fact. First, you watched Joseph and every skillful throw of his hammer; the way he ran his soot-covered hand through his black, curly hair; the way sweat raced and glistened on his dark skin. Then, you watched Mary as she went about her day—past guards and alleys in her hometown; the first time she chose a dress to wear and how the pearl-blue color of it twisted in the sun as she danced on the Sabbath. You watched their betrothal, and the wary, shy looks in their young eyes.

You were there when the angel spoke to Mary. You remember it all so well; it is not something you will ever forget. Mary woke with wide brown eyes. She scooted back in her bed in the corner of her room. Her cover fell from her knees, leaving them visible, two knobs of brown. Her sleeping gown was gold in the light of Gabrielle.

Gabrielle stood before Mary, though the angel seemed to float rather than stand. Her white robes flowed effortlessly around her. "Do not be afraid, Mary," Gabrielle said gently, slowly, "for you have found favor with God. You will conceive and give birth to a son, and you will name him Jesus."

You watched, over time, Mary's belly grow with righteous, holy life. Most importantly, though, you watched Joseph and Mary both as they traveled to Bethlehem.

That night was colder than usual, though not quite freezing. Still, puffs of white breath could be seen from the donkey's quivering lips.

Mary sat atop the donkey, one hand clasped to her stomach. Pain struck her there; her back, too. But she would not cry or complain.

You watch, because you have been commanded you cannot go near Joseph or Mary. They have been protected by God's hand; who are you to argue? Still, you are intrigued. Something about the life growing inside Mary calls to you, a beacon of hope and light. So you follow.

You follow Joseph and Mary house to house as they search, weary-footed and cold-bitten, for a spare room. They find not one. You cannot touch them, but you can encourage them. You let the wind get colder, to nip at their ears. They decide to stay in the only shelter available—a stable with hay scattered across its floor, which smells of dusty feed, of dirt-covered hooves, and matted fur.

There, Joseph carries Mary to a dip in the hay in the privacy of a stable stall. There, you follow her closely. Her water breaks, and panic fills her eyes. You hover, even, your hand close to her neck and the sweat and strained breath there. You want to brush the back of your fingers against her pulse and give her relief. But you will not.

Mary screams, filling the night with her labor. Joseph stays by her side, his hand wrapped in hers. White knuckles, sore muscles. They hold onto each other as their son is born.

That's when the night changes.

The cold breeze turns just a bit colder; in Bethlehem, it's out of the ordinary. But it's not unheard of. A stray cloud lets loose fragile drifts of snow before it goes on its way. Then another. Flecks of white fall outside. Puffs of warmth erupt from a few spectators who stand just outside the stable. As the sky clears in the midnight wind, a star is visible.

You look back to the child. He lies in Mary's arms, quiet as ever with eyes like hazelnuts and a rounded, pink nose.

Jesus looks between Mary and Joseph in awe, seeing through His human eyes for the first time. Then He looks at you. You have never seen anyone look directly at you before, but you know this is not just anyone. This is Jesus.

You will look Him in the eye again like this, if only for three days, then He will leave your company to fulfill the very reason for which he came.

With Resignation

There is a letter on the desk.

God's Spokesperson approaches. His robes swish around his blue ankles like the mist at the bottom of a tumultuous waterfall. The office around him is one that is infrequently visited. It's not off limits but simply feared.

It is furnished with dark wood and no windows. Tomes line the walls. There is only one chair—before which the letter is neatly fixed—and it's more of a throne than a chair. Angels with eyes covering their bodies are carved into the rich wood arch. The leather of the seat and back of the chair shines.

The Spokesperson rounds the table. He carefully takes in its contents—an unpainted clay cup that holds several pens of various styles from centuries past; a stack of plain white stationery paper and envelopes; a glass paperweight in the shape of a fruit with little air bubbles for seeds; a disposable white lighter; two skulls preserved in alarmingly pristine condition; a set of small, circular glasses with silver frames; and one silver spoon with streaks that imply it's been used and forgotten.

Then, there is the letter. It is written on the plain, white paper.

The Spokesperson sits.

A red feather quill rests across the letter as if it was not yet finished when its writer had gotten up to answer a needy call.

The Spokesperson moves the quill.

Dear Reader,
It's time.

As if that was all that needed to be written, the Spokesperson understands exactly what is meant by so few words. Even in the beginning, God was resigned to this fate.

In the end, He will have to destroy all that He created. It is something that all the angels—including the Spokesperson himself—know that God is not necessarily looking forward to. Still, it is a necessary destruction; it is inevitable.

That's when the Spokesperson feels the change. Somewhere in the distance, there is a great rumble, and the foundations of Heaven itself shake. A rupture follows—a crack that rattles the clay cup and pens inside. One of the skulls rolls onto the floor.

The Spokesperson rushes out. In the distance, where the white landscape stretches out and where buildings tuck into hazy mists, there is a blast of fire. Wings of flame flare upward. A pillar rises from the fire, and a fault line of red and embers divide the ground. Heaven's grounds split open, a crack in Earth's sky below.

Ashes flit down from Heaven's sky, and the Spokesperson knows that the Earth is experiencing its first rain of fire. It's the beginning of the end. *It's time.*

masterpiece

They will not remember who you are,
but history is already written in the stars.
It is a map to the faithful, braille to the blind,
the orchestral notes placed step by step by step,
the masterpiece God wove out of our lives.

acknowledgments

First, to God for giving me a life where I have the opportunity to chase my dreams and make books full of my art and writing.

Second, to the sheer determination it took to finish this collection.

Third, to the music that kept me alive in the process.

For craft writing itself, which has been a lifeline for surviving.

Then, to the friends who encouraged me through my lowest points; those who read my work and fawned over descriptions I wouldn't have otherwise noticed; those who understood the deeper meaning; those who listened to every draft and iteration of these worlds inside of me; those who gave me praise such as, *"riveting and perfect,"* that, on my worst days, kept me writing. Thank you.

A special thanks and a note: *With Resignation* was originally selected by F(r)iction Literary Magazine's *Dually Noted* series for publication in May 2023.

P.S. If you enjoyed the last four pieces—*stars*, Death Meets the Child of God, With Resignation, and *masterpiece*—I am excited to share that all these works exist inside of my fantasy series, Angels' Compass. Book one, *Inheriting Armageddon,* is out now.

about the author & artist

R. D. G. Lover is an artist, author, and freelancer. She owns a small business where she sells her original art and takes freelance work for editing services, website design, graphic design, custom paintings, and more. Lover spends her free time stargazing, singing loudly in her car, and working on her illustrated novels about the Four Horsemen of the Apocalypse. She has made it her goal to write and illustrate a novel in every genre.

Her website, www.4pocalypseArts.com, showcases a gallery of all-original art and writing from her stories. To stay up to date with R. D. G. Lover's future releases, be sure to subscribe to her newsletter on her website and follow her on any social media @4pocalypseArts.